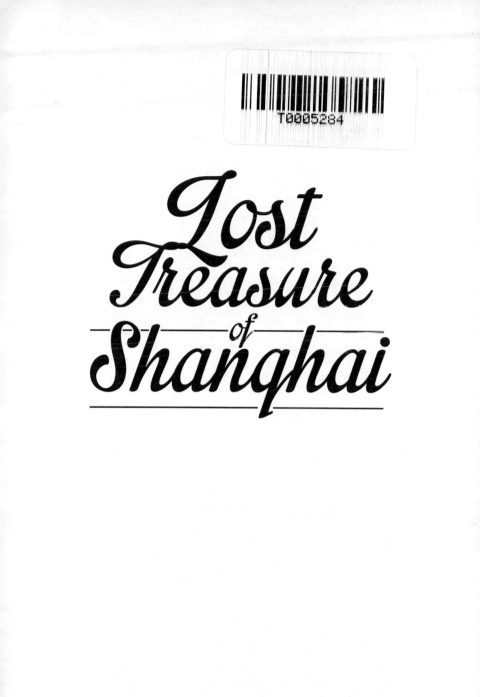

Lost Treasure of Shanghai

Lost Treasure of Shanghai

KIARA LOGANATHAN

TATE PUBLISHING
AND ENTERPRISES, LLC

Published by Tate Publishing & Enterprises, LLC
127 E. Trade Center Terrace | Mustang, Oklahoma 73064 USA
1.888.361.9473 | www.tatepublishing.com

Tate Publishing is committed to excellence in the publishing industry. The company reflects the philosophy established by the founders, based on Psalm 68:11,
"The Lord gave the word and great was the company of those who published it."

Book design copyright © 2013 by Tate Publishing, LLC. All rights reserved.
Cover design by Rodrigo Adolfo
Interior design by Jake Muelle

Published in the United States of America

ISBN: 978-1-62854-119-9
1. Fiction / Fantasy / Historical
2. Fiction / Action & Adventure
13.10.02

Dedication

I'd like to dedicate this book to my parents who encouraged me throughout the whole procedure of writing this book. Special thanks go to my mother who helped me study for my exams whilst writing this book and my father for helping me realize my dream. My inspiration for writing is accredited to my late grandfather who loved reading.

You can never dream too big or too small; it's what you want in life, and if you believe you can do it, you shall succeed, but with hard work....

Table of Contents

Dedication 5

The Beginning 9

The Emerald Dragon 12

The Coral Dragon 29

The Moonstone Dragon 45

The Sapphire Dragon 65

The Diamond Dragon 91

Journey Back Home 107

The Chamber 114

Arrested 129

The Beginning

Long ago in ancient China, near Shanghai, a twelve-year-old boy, Chang, lived with his elderly master, Lee. Lee had found Chang on his doorstep, raised the child as his own, and educated him. Chang grew into a curious and adventurous boy.

Chang and Lee lived deep in the forest, near a waterfall, far from the nearest village and the Shanghai palace where the great Emperor Wong and his beautiful daughter, Princess Xueman, lived. Her name meant "snowy grace." Chang had never seen the emperor or his daughter, but he always wondered about them.

One August night in 1875, Chang and Lee sat outside beside the fire where they were cooking their dinner.

"Master Lee, can you tell me the story of the lost treasure of Shanghai?" Chang pleaded. It was his favorite story.

"Sure." Lee smiled and began. "Long ago, when I was a young boy, Emperor Wong's father ruled the kingdom. I was only twelve years old, and Emperor Wong wasn't born yet. My father was employed as the emperor's adviser, and later that year, the emperor's soldiers went on a mission called the New Treasure of Shanghai. The emperor was informed that the treasure that was currently in the palace wasn't the true treasure. The soldiers searched the entire kingdom but failed to find it. The emperor cancelled the mission, and all the soldiers were summoned back to the palace. On their return, the soldiers saw a suspicious hooded person in the woods who was carrying a large, heavy sack. When the hooded person saw the soldiers approaching, he took off running. The soldiers gave chase, and just when the soldiers were about to catch him, he removed a big stone from his sack and threw it with all his might onto the ground. It broke into five pieces, momentarily startling the soldiers. This gave him a chance to run and hide in a nearby cave, where the soldiers were unable to find him. When the soldiers were gone, the hooded person came out to retrieve the pieces of the stone, but unfortunately, they had mysteriously disappeared."

Chang clapped his hands with excitement. "Tell me again…why did he have a stone?"

"It was not just a stone, it was the key to the true Treasure of Shanghai,"

"And how do you know that the stone was broken into five pieces?" Chang prompted although he already knew the answer.

"I was also a person who craved great adventures just like you. I wanted to retrieve the stone and find the real treasure of Shanghai, I was that hooded person," Lee said.

"Wow!" Chang exclaimed with a dreamy expression.

"Anyway, you need to go to bed so put the fire out," Lee said.

"Yes, Master," Chang bowed reverently.

The Emerald Dragon

Five Years Later

C hang grew into a responsible young man while
Master Lee became severely ill due to old age.
Chang was determined to find the lost treasure of
Shanghai but he was worried that his master might
die while he was gone. While Chang was sitting in his
master's room, Master Lee called him.

"Chang, there is something I never told you about
the lost treasure." Lee was breathing heavily, and Chang
held his hand firmly to comfort him. "There are two
maps in a box in my drawer. One will lead you to all five
pieces of the missing stone. Each piece is guarded by a
dragon. There are five dragons: the Emerald Dragon, the
Moonstone Dragon, the Diamond Dragon, the Coral
Dragon, and the Sapphire Dragon." Lee continued to
gasp for breath. "They all have metal armor from their
heads to their tails. In their armor on the forehead
are the stones. You will need to slay the dragons and
remove the stones. You must collect all five pieces and

bring them back to the palace chamber. The other map will lead you to the palace chamber. You must follow the instructions carefully.

"Please do this for me. Retrieve the lost treasure of Shanghai, and place it in the palace… and, Chang"— Master Lee gave him a weak but reassuring smile—"I will be with you every step you take." Master Lee let go of Chang's hand, took a deep breath, and closed his eyes.

When Chang started to cry, Master Lee slowly opened his eyes and kidded, "I am not dead, dummy." And Lee closed his eyes again.

Once again, Chang started to cry.

Master Lee mumbled, "Silly boy, I'm not dead, I'm just tired."

"Sorry, Master," Chang apologized.

"You better not be, trying to kill me off early," Master Lee chuckled to himself.

The next day, Chang awoke and went to his master's bedroom. He tried to wake his master up, but he wouldn't budge. This time, his master was indeed dead. In the afternoon, Chang buried his master, lit incense, and placed flowers on his grave, promising that he would fulfill his master's wish.

Chang remembered the map, went into his master's bedroom, found the box, and went outside to sit by the fire. He opened the box and saw two maps: one for the stones and the other for the chamber. Chang carefully studied the maps and resolved that in the morning he would set out on his journey. Chang placed the maps back in the box, looked at his master's grave, and whispered, "Master, I wish you were here to accompany me on my adventure." Tears started to build up in Chang's eyes, but he stopped them from falling.

The next morning, when Chang awoke and opened the box, he found another piece of paper that said Master Lee owned a horse in the village.

Chang dressed and went to the village, which was a very busy place. He reread the piece of paper to confirm the address and the name of the person who had the horse.

Chang arrived at the address, situated in the rich part of the village. He saw a man on the premises, walked up to him, and politely asked, "Are you Shen?"

"Yes, I am he, and who are you?" Shen looked his visitor up and down.

"I am Chang, the apprentice of Master Lee." Chang bowed.

"Oh, my old friend, Master Lee," Shen brightened. "Nice man, wise. How is he?"

"He passed away yesterday," Chang frowned.

"I am so sorry to hear that," Shen shook his head sadly. "And why are you here?"

"I came for his horse, and I have a piece of paper to prove it," Chang said.

"Show me the paper," Shen held out his hand.

Chang gave him the piece of paper and Shen walked to his barn. Five minutes later, he came out leading a beautiful black Arabian.

"Chang, this horse is the daughter of Master Lee's original horse who died. Feed her only fresh grass, fruit, and water daily," Shen instructed Chang.

"Okay, thank you, Shen," Chang nodded.

"Before you go, here is Lee's equipment for the horse." Shen handed Chang the saddle, bridle, and reins he was holding in his other hand. "And you are welcome anytime to my place."

Chang thanked him, but before he turned to leave, he asked Shen, "What is her name?"

"She is called Black Beauty, but you can change the name if you want."

"No." Chang shook his head. "I'll keep the name, and thanks again, Shen."

"You are welcome, young man," Shen smiled.

Chang admired Black Beauty all the way home. Chang tied Black Beauty's reins around a post and gave her fresh food and water. Chang would set out the next day to find the stones and retrieve the lost treasure of Shanghai. He packed all the things that he'd need such as food, water, and clothes for the journey.

Morning arrived and Chang went to saddle up Black Beauty. He placed the maps in his hip pocket and they proceeded on their journey. After hours of traveling in the forest, evening fell. Chang was tired and camped out for the night in an open clearing near a lake.

Chang relieved Black Beauty of her baggage, removing the saddle and supplies off her back. Chang caught a fish and roasted it over the fire for dinner.

The next morning, Chang awoke to find Back Beauty was gone. He called out her name, starting to panic, and searched around the forest. He finally found her eating fruit from a tree far from the campsite. Chang breathed a sigh of relief, then lead Black Beauty back to the camp. Chang, both relieved and thirsty, drank some water from the lake. He then saddled up Black Beauty, secured the supplies on her back, and started their journey for the day.

Around midday, Chang took a rest, which also allowed Black Beauty to graze in the forest. Chang took out the map to study it and ensure they were on the right path to the Emerald Dragon.

By evening, Chang and Black Beauty were much deeper in the forest than he had ever been before. When rain started to fall, Chang was lucky to spot a cave where they could take cover and rest for the night.

Chang made a fire to keep warm, but he did not cook anything to eat in order to preserve his supplies. Black Beauty was resting nearby as Chang removed the map to study it further, and the flickering of the fire revealed a drawing on the cave wall that caught his attention. Chang got up for a closer view. The drawing depicted five dragons; to the left of the picture, Master Lee's name was inscribed. Chang realized that this was probably the cave his master had mentioned in the story he'd often narrated to him as a young boy. Chang went to sleep, excited and couldn't wait for the night to end to continue his journey.

In the morning, Chang was disappointed to see the heavy rainfall had not let up. He knew they couldn't travel in such bad weather, so he went back over and compared both the map and the drawings on the wall. The dragons were colored in different shades, allowing Chang to identify each of them. Light green represented the Emerald Dragon. Light orange was the Coral Dragon. White represented the Moonstone Dragon. Light blue was the Sapphire Dragon, and grey represented the Diamond Dragon. He was also able to figure out which piece of the stone each dragon represented. The Emerald Dragon had the top left piece. The Coral Dragon had the top right piece. The Moonstone Dragon had the bottom left piece. The Sapphire Dragon had the bottom right piece, and the Diamond Dragon had the middle piece. The assembled stones represented the shape of a diamond.

Chang put his map away and studied the drawings intensely. He realized the drawing reflected that the Emerald, Coral, Moonstone and Sapphire Dragons were all the same size; but the Diamond Dragon was double the size of all four other dragons. Chang sat down on the ground and wondered to himself, *How am I going to slay all five dragons? And how especially am I supposed to slay the biggest dragon? How am I going to retrieve the pieces of the stone that are encrusted in the armor of the dragons?* Chang had many questions to ask, but he had no one else to talk to but Black Beauty. After an hour, the rain stopped. Chang strapped all his supplies onto Black Beauty and continued on his journey farther into the forest. Around mid-afternoon, Chang decided to rest his horse. While Black Beauty was enjoying her grazing and Chang was making himself familiar with his surroundings, the quietness of the forest was disturbed by a loud roar. It was louder than a lion's roar or any other wildcat. Chang panicked and quietly called out to Black Beauty. The horse gently trotted back to

Chang. He quickly mounted and hurriedly left, afraid he could be attacked by wild animals.

They proceeded deeper into the forest as Chang tried to calm his nerves. He pulled out the map to ensure they were traveling in the right direction toward the Emerald Dragon. He traced his finger over the map and realized he was not far from his first quest.

Chang was putting away the map when he noticed several human footprints on the ground. He got off his horse and followed the prints like a tracker to see where they would lead, wondering to himself, *Why would anyone come this deep into the forest? Do they live here?* An hour of tracking lead him to a group of thin, ragged, unfriendly, dangerous-looking men camping together. Chang was worried about approaching them. *What if they are thieves or treasure hunters?*

In the end, he put his fears aside and walked up to the campsite. He introduced himself but didn't tell the people the reason for his journey or why he and Black Beauty were so deep in the forest, and all alone. He asked the leader of the group, Meng, if he could spend the night with them. Meng wanted to be compensated for accommodating Chang.

"What do I have to give in return?" Chang said with apprehension, asking curiously.

"How about that Arabian?" Meng raised a greedy eyebrow.

"Sorry, I can't give this horse up, she is my only companion and friend." Chang shook his head resolutely. "But is there anything else you want in return?"

"I will take anything else that is worth much more than this beauty." Meng grinned, showing several missing teeth.

Chang had to think quickly…something that was worth more than his Black Beauty…he remembered the box that held Master Lee's old maps. "Yes, I have something worth more than my horse."

"Okay, let's see, shall we?" Meng held out his calloused hand.

Chang retrieved the intricately carved box from his supply bag and showed the man. Meng's eyes widened; he quickly snatched the box from Chang's hand and confirmed Chang's stay for the night.

The next morning, Chang thanked the man for the accommodation and proceeded on his journey. He removed the map from his pocket to look for a landmark to ensure that he was on the right path toward the waterfall. After several hours of traveling, Chang could hear rapidly falling water in the far distance. Excitement rose in his chest, and he followed the sound of the falling water. It took him another hour to reach the waterfall; it was a low, cool fall, with sparkling water flowing over the rocks and cascading into a crystal clear pool below.

Chang jumped off Black Beauty, removed the supplies and the saddle, and decided to set up camp for the night on the banks of the waterfall. The water was looking inviting, and it had been a long time since he took a decent bath. Chang undressed and dove in while his horse sipped the cool water from the banks and munched on the lush green vegetation around it. While swimming, Chang managed to catch a fish for dinner.

The swim left Chang feeling refreshed; he started a fire to cook his dinner and to keep him warm for the night. After dinner, Chang lay on his back observing the starry night, and thinking of his master, he slowly drifted off to sleep. In his dream he and his master were sitting in his room. Chang was listening to all Master Lee's adventure stories in his younger days. All of a sudden, he heard soldiers approaching his master's house. Chang bolted upright with fright, cold sweat running down his face, only to realize he was in the middle of the forest, alone with his horse on the banks of the waterfall.

Chang took out both maps and opened the one to the palace chamber. The map revealed a complex route laden with traps and bogus detours. However, the notes on the map stated that the safest route to the palace chambers was from under the palace. Chang was confused, unable to find the safe entrance on the map. He kept repeating in his head, *How am I going to go under the palace? Master, please help me?* After a few minutes, it dawned upon him. He turned the map upside down and clear as daylight the entrance to the palace was revealed.

"You clever old man," Chang uttered under his breath. He put both the maps away and fell asleep. In the morning, Chang collected some fresh water for his journey and remembered the next landmark on his map was a village, which was a day's journey away from the waterfall. Chang estimated that they would reach that village by late afternoon.

Hours of traveling led Chang to a watering hole, and a good place to rest for a while. It occurred to him that before he reached the next village, he needed to find something valuable to trade for his stay with the villagers. He rummaged through his belongings and found the golden ring his master had given him. Chang felt that this was more valuable than his Arabian. He held the ring in his hand and thought of the good times he'd had with his master and the lost treasure story he'd heard so often. He placed the ring safely in his pocket to offer a trade if need be.

Chang had just calculated his journey to the Emerald Dragon to be six days away when he was disturbed by a loud roar, similar to the one he'd heard a couple days back. *Is it the roar of the dragon? Or is it some other dangerous forest animal?*

All went quiet again, and he breathed a sigh of relief. He reminded himself, *If I retrieve the lost treasure of Shanghai, my master will indeed be proud of me.* He then remembered those few words his master told him a day before he died. "I will be with you every step you take." His master's voice rang in his head.

It was a short distance to reach the village. Chang knew he would have to risk his life to retrieve the lost treasure, but he viewed this adventure as a worthy challenge. While walking along the path, he came across a wolf puppy. He halted Black Beauty and tied her to a tree. Chang picked up the pup and went in search of the mother. He walked around a bush and saw the mother laying down dead with another puppy urgently tugging on its mother's hind leg. Chang picked up the other pup, took them with him, and placed them on Black beauty in a little bag. The horse was calm when he placed the two pups on her, as if she didn't mind at all. Chang returned to the bush with a small shovel from his supply bag and buried the pups' mother.

Chang took the pups out of the bag, placed them under each arm, and continued his journey. It was late afternoon when he reached the village. He approached the village chief to seek permission to stay the night. He asked if the chief would accommodate his horse, the puppies, and himself for the night. The chief was an old, wrinkled man who had been through many of life's challenges, yet his eyes were warm and inviting and spoke in a gentle and respectable tone of voice and seems to have the respect of his people.

The Chief welcomed his party, and Chang quietly asked, "Do you require anything in return?"

The chief let loose a benevolent smile and replied, "You may stay for the night, and I don't wish anything in return."

Chang was offered a small hut to stay and his horse was placed in a stable for the night. Chang was given a warm meal by the villagers and he shared it with the puppies who devoured the food hungrily. After dinner, the chief questioned Chang about his journey and he replied honestly to the chief that he was out there to search for the missing treasure of Shanghai.

In the morning, before Chang could leave, the chief gave him a basket that he could secure onto Black

Beauty and place the puppies into. The villagers also provided a small basket of food for his journey. Chang thanked the villagers and the chief for their generosity. Before he could leave, the chief presented Chang with a gleaming sword and said, "Take this for protection."

Chang tied the sword around his waist, climbed on his horse, said his farewells to the villagers, and proceeded on his journey. It was not very long before dark clouds began to gather. Black Beauty was getting restless as if she could smell a storm approaching. Chang quickly searched for a suitable shelter to shield the puppies, horse, and himself from the oncoming storm. He managed to locate a cave that had just enough space for all of them. Just then, the thunder rumbled, and the lightning became intense and rapid. The puppies were scared and ran to Chang for protection. The rain pelted down severely, and the temperature began to drop. Chang started a fire to keep themselves warm until the storm died down.

For over three hours, they had been stuck in the cave and Chang was becoming restless. He took out the map to check the progress made so far, and he realized that the rain was severely delaying his journey to find the Emerald Dragon. It was late evening before the rain stopped. Chang felt he was sufficiently rested and opted to travel at night to catch up with lost time.

They trudged throughout the night without stopping, and when morning arrived, Chang took a short break to feed himself and allow Black Beauty to graze. The puppies were playing nearby while Chang went into deep thought, hearing his master's voice again, saying, "I will be with you every step you take." It kept on ringing in his head until he was disturbed by sounds of barking. Chang roused from his slumber and took out the map to gauge the distance of the final landmark before he would reach the dragon's lair. He estimated a day's travel to the final landmark, which was another waterfall.

Chang continued his journey until he reached the waterfall. He was extremely tired and realized that he needed a long rest before he could take on the Emerald Dragon; furthermore, he also needed to have a plan of attack in slaying the dragon. He took out an apple the villagers gave him, and just before he could bite into it, he felt Black Beauty's cold nose on the back of his head. He realized that Black Beauty wanted something other than grass. Chang placed the apple on the palm of his hand, and the horse gently ate it. Chang then took out the sword he was given by the village chief to admire its beauty. The handle was gold encrusted with gems, and the blade was double-edged and shiny. Chang figured the best time to attack the dragon was just after midday because it would have eaten and fallen off to sleep.

In the morning, Chang changed into his master's clan clothes: black in color with the symbol of a serpent on the back of the shirt and sweatband. He burnt incense and offered prayers to his ancestors and his master and requested their guidance and help for him to conquer the Emerald Dragon. He then left some food and water for the puppies and Black Beauty and asked her to look after the puppies until he got back. He was sure she understood what he had said, for she nodded her head and neighed. Chang placed the sword on the side of his waist secured by a belt then placed two small sacks in his pocket to place the stone and gem in after retrieving them from the dragon.

Chang scaled the mountain on which the dragon lived. He was not at all nervous. He took deep breaths to clear his mind and to stay focused. Chang slowly approached the opening of the cave, and he could hear the dragon snoring loudly. He slowly removed his sword and held it firmly in front of him and started to tiptoe into the cave.

He got his first glimpse of the dragon and was shocked at the size of it. In his mind he shouted out, *This is a huge dragon! How am I going to slay him?* Just then, a little voice in his head told Chang, *Be calm and stay focused and remember what the master has taught you.*

The dragon was without a doubt huge with light green scales, metal armor from his forehead to his tail that was in the shape of a diamond. On the forehead, a huge emerald stone was embedded in the armor, and below it was a piece of the stone his master had mentioned to him in his story. This was indeed the Emerald Dragon and the first dragon according to the map.

With the Emerald Dragon in a deep slumber, Chang thought, *It will be easy to slay this dragon, then get the gem and the stone.*

Or so he thought, for the dragon's snout twitched, and his eyes opened slowly. The Emerald Dragon was now staring directly at Chang. It rose up to its full height and roared fiercely while violently flapping his wings.

Chang took cover behind a rock. The Emerald Dragon's roar was ear-piercingly loud and Chang heard a deep, gruff voice, "Who enters my cave and wakes me from my slumber?"

Chang came out from behind the rock. "It is I, Chang, the apprentice of the late Master Lee."

The dragon looked down at Chang. "What have you come here for?"

"I am here for the stone and the gem that is encrusted in your armor," Chang bravely said.

"Ha! I will not give it to you. I was tasked to protect it. You would have to slay me first in order to retrieve those two objects, the stone and the gem," the dragon proudly replied.

"Let us make it easy." Chang shrugged. "You just give me the stone and the gem, I don't have to slay you, and we both live."

"Have it your way, we will fight!" the dragon shouted, spewing short streak of fire.

The Emerald Dragon became furious and swayed his tail vigorously back and forth. Chang tried to stab the dragon's tail, but he missed. Chang was looking for a weak spot within the dragon's armor and couldn't spot one, but he had an idea. *If I can go under the dragon's belly and stab him, the dragon will become weak and fall to the ground. Then I could climb on him and I'll be able to reach the dragon's head.*

The dragon became more agitated and started to breathe long jets of emerald fire. Chang quickly took cover behind a rock to avoid being toasted. He found and threw a rock away from him to create a distraction. When the dragon turned its head, Chang quickly slipped underneath the belly of the beast and plunged his sword into its soft underbelly.

The dragon screeched in pain, and Chang jumped onto its back and climbed up to the head of the dragon. While it was twisting in pain, Chang held on tightly. He managed to reach the dragon's head safely and wrapped his legs around the dragon's neck tightly, then he stuck his sword firmly through the dragon's head.

The dragon screeched and roared in pain as he fell with a mighty thump to the ground. Chang removed the emerald stone from its forehead; just then he heard rumbling sounds and looked up to see the ceiling of the cave starting to crumble. With all his might, he yanked both of the stones free and ran out of the cave just as it collapsed, shaking the earth and burying the emerald dragon with it.

Chang returned to his campsite completely exhausted and covered with bruises. He went over to the waterfall and had a cool and refreshing drink before dropping down next to Black Beauty, satisfied and happy that he had completed his first quest successfully.

He attended to his scars and scratches with some herbal medication he'd made back home. When evening fell, he made a fire to prepare his dinner, he then fed both Black Beauty the puppies and lay there peacefully with his eyes closed, awaiting eagerly for the night to end so that he can get going. In his mind, he was wondering what challenges and obstacles await him and what he will encounter on his way to finding the Coral Dragon, but he couldn't tell the future so he had to wait and see.

The Coral Dragon

When morning arrived, Chang felt something warm, furry, and heavy on his stomach. He looked down to discover that one of the puppies was curled up and fast asleep. He carefully picked up the puppy and laid him on the ground beside him without disturbing him. Chang stretched out his body, and it was still sore. He freshened up, and with his confidence booming, he wanted to get an early start to locate the next dragon on the map, the Coral Dragon.

Chang pulled out the map to plan his route. As he opened it, he saw that the Emerald Dragon had vanished from the page. He scratched his head and uttered, "Is this a magical map?" He then checked to ensure that the emerald and the piece of rock were securely placed in a secret compartment of his bag.

Within minutes, Black Beauty was saddled up and all his supplies were packed. Chang placed the two puppies in the basket and continued his journey. Chang estimated the Coral Dragon to be about five days' ride without experiencing any delays.

While traveling, Chang began daydreaming about Master Lee and Princess Xueman. He was thinking about how his master had taught him martial arts, to read and write, and how he'd described the beautiful Princess Xueman, with a jasmine flower placed in her long, silky black hair and her long silk dress and her necklace with a golden dragon pedant, which she would never take off.

Just then, he was disturbed by the barking of the puppies. Chang looked to see what all the fuss was about, only to see them perched on the edge of the basket and barking at a wild pig in the nearby bushes. Chang realized this was dinner; he slowly climbed off Black Beauty, pulled out his dagger, took aim, and threw it at the pig. The dagger pierced the pig in the stomach, and it started to run around aimlessly squealing in pain. Chang took out his sword, gave chase, and put an end to the pig's misery.

Chang whispered to the pig, "You will be my dinner for the next few days." Chang thanked the puppies for being alert and told them, "Tonight we are having roast pork for dinner." The puppies looked at him confused, as if to say, "Whatever."

Chang camped out the night where he slew the pig. He cut up the pig, took the meat he required, and left the remainder for any hungry animals that were in need of food. Chang then went in search of some wood, leaving the puppies in the care of Black Beauty. He returned with the wood, and soon the fire was glowing brightly in the dark surroundings. Chang roasted some meat over the fire and shared it with the puppies. As he was cleaning up and preparing his camp for the night, one of the puppies started to howl. Chang turned around to see it was gazing up at the sky; he realized wolves like to howl at the full moon. Chang took out the map to locate the next landmark, which was a spring, then put the map away and lay down for the night.

When morning arrived, he packed for his journey. The weather was not looking good; the wind was strong, and it blew sand into their faces. Chang tied a length of cloth around his nose and mouth and proceeded through the wind. The puppies, fast asleep in the basket, were oblivious to the windstorm. Chang shook his head and said to Black Beauty, "Maybe, the pups are just tired."

The horse nodded her head and neighed in agreement.

After a demanding journey, Chang reached the spring. It was surrounded by lush vegetation, tall trees, and the spring was whistling softly into an inviting pond. Chang was unsaddling his horse when he heard a rustling sound. He pulled out his sword and scanned the area for danger but he could see none. Just as Chang was about to relax, he heard a growl, and fear set in. It was a similar to the growl he'd heard some weeks ago. "Am I being followed?" Chang worried aloud.

The growling appeared to be getting closer, and Chang rallied his horse and puppies around him; they, too, were scared. Suddenly, the bushes parted and a tiger appeared. Now Chang was scared sick from head to toes; he stood frozen with fear.

Thinking quickly, he reached into his supply sack, took out a piece of meat, and said, "Here, nice tiger, are you hungry? How about *this* instead of me?"

The tiger roared, causing Chang to drop his sword and the meat; he instinctively ran behind Black Beauty. Then, a voice said, "Sorry, young boy, I didn't mean to scare you. I just have an irritating hairball that simply won't come out."

Chang emerged from behind Black Beauty and came face-to-face with the tiger.

"You can talk?" Chang asked, surprised.

"Yes, all the animals in the forest can talk," the tiger replied.

"Then how come my horse and my wolf puppies don't talk?" Chang challenged him.

The tiger shook his head. "Your Arabian doesn't come from the forest, and you are not too bright if you do not know that those puppies are still too young. They won't be able to talk until they are a year old, so be patient."

Chang returned a sheepish grin.

"What is your name?" the tiger asked.

"I am Chang, the apprentice of the late Master Lee," he said with pride.

"He was a good man," the tiger acknowledged.

"You knew him?" Chang said, surprised.

"No, I never met him, but I know he was an excellent man, and he must have treated you like his son."

"What is your name?" Chang inquired.

"I am called Eel," the tiger replied.

"Eel?" Chang let loose a giggle. "Why do you have a sea creature's name?"

"You will soon find out later," the tiger said mysteriously. "So what brings you so deep in the forest and far away from home?"

"I am here to find all five dragons, slay all five, get the gems, and get the pieces of the stone," Chang said matter-of-factly.

"I'm guessing that you have killed the Emerald Dragon?" Eel postulated.

"Yes." Chang's jaw fell open. "How do you know?"

"I know everything that happens in this forest," Eel said then made a sad face for effect.

"Yes?" Chang picked up the cue.

"Do you mind taking in an old, helpless, harmless tiger?" Eel asked.

"That depends," Chang eyed him warily. "I'd be glad to have you along, but can you walk and run far distances?"

"Yes, of course I can." Eel rolled his eyes.

"Welcome, to my family, Eel!" Chang smiled brightly.

"Don't you think we should make a fire? I'm starving, and I'll bet you and your companions are as well," Eel suggested.

"Thanks for the tip," Chang nodded. He picked his sword up and put it away then quickly gathered some wood and started a fire.

The puppies and Black Beauty were fed, and they lay down for the night. Chang and Eel shared some of the roasted pig.

"You are a brave boy to come so deep in the forest to try to slay all the dragons and retrieve the lost treasure of Shanghai," Eel commented.

"Thank you, Eel, but may I ask again how come your name is—"

Eel interrupted before Chang could complete his sentence. "Like I told you before…you will soon find out."

"Wait a minute," Chang suddenly remembered, "the wild pig that I killed yesterday didn't talk."

"He isn't from this forest, either," Eel replied.

"Oh," Chang said.

Eel took a moment to look Chang up and down then said, "Come here."

"Why?" Chang asked warily.

"No questions, just come here," Eel said.

Chang moved next to the tiger and Eel said, "Show me all you scars and bruises."

"Why?" Chang still didn't trust Eel.

"Just show me," Eel snapped.

Chang removed his clothes as necessary; he flinched when Eel took his tongue and began to lick the various scars and bruises. As he did so, each one disappeared. Chang was shocked!

"H-how d-did y-you…?" Chang stammered.

Eel laughed and said, "Get some shut-eye and I'll tell you tomorrow."

Chang took out his grass mat and made his bed for the night.

Unknown to Chang, Eel stayed awake the entire night watching over Chang and, at one point, whispered to him, "Like I told you before, *I will be with you every step you take.*"

After he said those words, a smile appeared on Chang's face. He knew that even though Chang was fast asleep, those words would ring in his head.

When morning arrived, Chang packed away his supplies, placed the puppies in the basket, and jumped on Black Beauty. Eel was standing beside Black Beauty when Chang looked down and asked, "Are you able to walk far today?"

"Of course." Eel looked up at him with a scowl.

They started to walk slowly at first until Chang had a mischievous thought. He instructed Black Beauty to gallop a bit faster so that he can test the old tiger. To his surprise, the tiger outran him.

Chang stopped and Eel snorted, "Do not think you are so smart. I might be old, but these bones are strong."

Chang laughed out loud, and from then on, they both walked side by side. Chang was enjoying Eel's company as it oddly reminded him of Master Lee.

When late afternoon came, Eel remarked, "Why don't you look at the map and locate the next landmark that you want to reach?"

"Good idea," Chang said, retrieving the map. Chang studied the map and saw there was some kind of a village not so far away from where they were standing. Chang estimated the distance, saying, "Eel, I think we'll reach this village on the map by the evening."

"Let's say that we'll reach that village in the early hours of the morning," Eel corrected him.

"Whatever you say," Chang mumbled to himself, making a funny face when Eel turned around.

"Mind that attitude, boy," Eel cautioned him.

"But, but, but, h-how did you...when your back was..." Chang stammered.

"Like I told you before, I know about *everything* that happens in the forest—including people," Eel replied.

"But, but, but..." Chang stammered again.

"Are we going to walk or just stand around and stammer all day?" Eel pointed his head in the direction of the village.

"Yeah, I think so we should go," Chang said, still somewhat shocked.

While Chang put the map away, Eel took off, walking fast and shouting over his shoulder, "Chang, c'mon, step on it!"

When night fell, they were still walking. The only sounds that could be heard in the night were Black Beauty's hooves and the crickets rubbing their legs together. Eel, who was up ahead, shouted back at Chang, "We are nearly there. We just have three hours to go!"

"How do you know?" Chang called out.

"I can sense it," Eel shouted back.

"Whatever you say," Chang mumbled to himself.

"Mind that attitude, boy!" Eel shouted.

Chang cringed. "Seriously! You've got to stop doing that!"

"Chang!" Eel remonstrated.

"Sorry, Eel!" Chang replied softly.

"That's more like it!" Eel nodded.

They walked without stopping until two and a half hours had gone by when Chang and Eel saw something in the near distance.

Eel said excitedly, "The village is just up ahead!"

"Yeah, I think I see it," Chang replied.

It was early morning, and the village was quiet. An elderly lady emerged from behind a huge hut, and they walked over to her.

"Hi, name's Chang," he began the introductions. "And this is my Arabian, Black Beauty, these are my puppies, and this is my tiger friend, Eel. Don't worry, he's a harmless, old, helpless tiger. Anyway, I was wondering if we could rest here in the village for a while?"

"Welcome, Chang." The old lady smiled. "But this is not a village. All these huts are mine. This is my home, and I also have an old, harmless, helpless tiger. I'm not sure if your tiger talks, but mine does. You are welcome to stay for as long as you want."

"Thank you." Chang bowed to her. "May I ask what your name is?"

"My name is Ming," she responded, "which means *shiny*."

"Nice to meet you, Ming," Chang said.

Chang and Black Beauty walked on ahead, but Eel hesitated and his sixth sense told him she was from the dark side. He looked at the old lady and growled at her as if to say that her intentions were evil. The old lady's eyes then turned yellow and she hissed, sending Eel quickly running after Chang. Eel was convinced that something was not right; he tried to talk Chang, but all that came out of his mouth was a growling sound.

Chang was confused. "What is the matter, Eel?"

Once again, Eel tried to speak but all that came out of his mouth was growling.

Chang shook his head. "Suit yourself. If you don't want to talk to me, fine."

Eel was confused, he then realized that the old lady had placed a spell on him when her eyes turned yellow, and that she was up to no good.

Just then, the old lady caught up with them and asked, "Is there something wrong?"

"No," Chang said in frustration. "It's just that my tiger, he won't talk to me—now all he's doing is growling."

Ming wagged her head to show she understood. "My tiger does the same thing. Why don't you walk ahead to that big cottage and I'll catch up."

"Okay," Chang replied.

As Chang and Black Beauty were nearing the cottage, Eel looked at Ming and growled as loud as he could. Even the birds were frightened and flew off.

Chang turned around and asked Ming, "Is something wrong?"

"Everything's fine," she replied. "I'm just talking to Eel and he seems to be upset, but don't worry, I'll take care of it. You just carry on to that big cottage with that beauty of a horse."

Eel growled at Ming again, showing his sharp teeth.

Ming hissed back, "I hope I taught you a lesson on respect."

Eel growled once more then hurried to Chang. "We have to leave. This is not a safe place to stay. We better go find another place to camp!"

"Eel, you are talking nonsense." Chang chuckled. "But at least you're talking now."

"Chang, listen to me. This old lady and this tiger of hers are snakes!" Eel exclaimed.

"Eel, stop being rude," Chang waved him off.

"Chang, she placed a brief spell on me so I couldn't talk. I do not think it is a good idea to hang around here any longer," Eel explained.

"Eel, I want you to stop it. This place is perfectly fine. Ming and her tiger are not snakes," Chang raised his voice. "Do you understand me?!"

"Did you forget? I know everything that happens in this forest—and I know that Ming and her tiger are snakes!" Eel exclaimed.

"I don't want to hear any of this nonsense again. Discussion over!" Chang said with finality.

Chang was tired and wanted to sleep. He suggested, "Eel, if you are afraid of Ming, do you think you can stay up the whole night and keep watch?"

"Believe me, I will," Eel said with a serious look on his face.

"If anything happens, just growl," Chang said.

"Okay," Eel replied.

After a few hours, Eel growled softly in Chang's ear. Chang shook his head and went back to sleep. Eel growled a little louder. Chang rose up with a fright and said, "What did you get me up for!?"

"Ssshhhh… Listen carefully. Can you hear that hissing sound?" Eel whispered.

"Yeah, I can." Chang hopped to his feet. "Let's check it out."

Chang strapped on his sword and followed the sound until they met up with Ming and her tiger who were seated outside their dimly lit hut within the village.

"Hi, Ming. What are you doing?" Chang asked.

"I was feeling a little bit hungry, and I was wondering if I can have you for dinner?" Ming said with an evil grin on her face. Her eyes were as yellow as a snake's eyes.

"Yeah, sure," Chang replied in a playful way.

"I hope you don't mind, but my tiger has sharp teeth so you might have a painful death," Ming cackled with the same evil grin.

In the next moment, Ming and her tiger changed into two huge king cobras. Chang's mouth dropped wide open.

"Great, snakes! I hate snakes! Why didn't you tell me that they were snakes?!" Chang shouted at Eel.

"I did tell you, but you ignored me, and now thanks to you for not listening, we have to slay not one but two king cobras!" Eel shouted back.

Ming hissed at Chang, "C'mon, I don't have all day."

The two snakes attacked, but Eel was fast and slashed Ming's tail off with his sharp claws. Chang stood temporarily frozen by his fear of snakes. Ming lunged at Chang, and at the last possible second, he swung his sword hard and severed her head. As he was about to celebrate his victory, a new head grew out of the same body. His grin was wiped off his face. Chang exclaimed, "Eel!" How is it possible that her head grew back and now her body is longer?!"

Eel was busy fighting the other snake but replied, "You see, since these two are magical creatures, they need to be killed at the same time in order for them to die!"

Chang shouted, "I got a plan to slay these two snakes. We need to start slashing them from the tail upward, together."

"Okay!" Eel shouted back.

They carried out their plan, and just before they reached the head of both snakes, Ming and her tiger burst into flames and vanished. Chang and Eel were surprised by what had taken place, but they were also glad to be rid of the deadly creatures.

They both retired to the cottage for the night, and just before Chang could doze off, he took out his map. And before his eyes, the village disappeared from the page. Chang looked on in amazement. "Eel? How is it possible that whenever I slay a beast, the landmark on the map disappears?"

"That is a map of a magical forest," Eel replied.

"But…" Chang started, but he was interrupted.

"I will tell you tomorrow." Eel yawned. "So blow out the candle because tomorrow is going to be a long and hard day."

Chang fell off to sleep, but Eel stayed awake the whole night, protecting them in case any more danger came. When morning arrived, Chang once again took out the map to estimate the distance to the Coral Dragon, only to realize he was only a few hours away.

Chang turned to Eel. "Why didn't you tell me that we were so close to the Coral Dragon?"

"Well, I did," Eel replied.

"No, you didn't!" Chang exclaimed.

"What? Didn't you understand 'tomorrow is gonna be a long and hard day'?" Eel raised his eyebrows.

"Oh," Chang said and went quiet.

"We better get going if we want to slay that Coral Dragon," Eel suggested.

"Yeah, we should," Chang nodded his head.

They continued their journey, and shortly, they were in a canyon with a lot of sharp and pointed rocks all over. The ground was covered in sand the color of dark chocolate. It was a hot and humid day. Chang was already sweating even though he hadn't started his battle yet. Chang and Eel looked for a safe place among the rocks to hide Black Beauty and the puppies.

Eel and Chang then ventured forth to find the Coral Dragon that lived nearby. They soon heard a loud, heavy flapping sound; they turned around to see a huge orange dragon with armor from head to tail. On its forehead was a coral stone embedded in the armor.

The dragon was furious and demanded, "Why do you enter my canyon?"

"We are here to retrieve that stone around your neck, and the gemstone that is encased in your armor," Chang replied without showing any fear.

"Who are you?" the Coral Dragon barked.

"I am Chang, the apprentice of the late Master Lee, and this is my pet tiger, Eel."

"Eel? The animal who thinks he knows everything—who thinks he is the king of this forest? You are wrong! Us five dragons are the kings of this forest!" the Coral Dragon growled.

"Okay, since you said that all the dragons know what goes on in this forest, I am sure you already know that your dear brother, the Emerald Dragon, has been killed by this young boy?" Eel challenged.

"What? The Emerald Dragon is dead?" the dragon exclaimed, and with great anger, he bellowed out a loud roar that shook the canyon walls. I will kill all of you for this!" And the dragon blew orange fire through his nostrils.

Eel was quick to react and placed a magical shield between the dragon and themselves to prevent them from being burnt. Just before the dragon could blast out another flame, Eel quickly attacked the dragon's belly. Chang tried to chop off the tail with his sword, but he was hit with it as it swayed from side to side, and he fell to the ground. Chang got up, attacked the tail once again while Eel was attacking its belly. Chang managed to stab the dragon's tail several times with his sword, and the dragon screeched in pain; then it became more aggressive.

Eel called out to Chang to attack the dragon's belly. The tiger distracted the dragon by biting its legs while Chang slipped unnoticed underneath the dragon and plunged his sword several times into its belly.

As the dragon was squealing in pain, the vibration of its roar started the sharp, jagged rocks above them to break loose. A large rock with a sharp point broke off and was falling rapidly toward the dragon. It stabbed him through his armor, and he fell to the ground with a loud thud.

Chang plunged his sword just below the dragon's neck to ensure it was once and for all dead. The dragon let out a final loud screech, then it went silent with blood flowing down the canyon.

Eel removed the stone from around its neck while Chang used his sword to remove the coral stone from the armor on the dragon's forehead.

"We must thank the gods for this," Eel called out to Chang.

"Yes, thank the gods for the rock that pierced the dragon, otherwise we'd still be in battle," Chang replied happily.

"Let's get out of here and enjoy a well-deserved rest and a meal," Eel suggested. "But first let's make sure the gems are well secured."

They completed their task then headed back to camp where Black Beauty and the puppies awaited their return.

The Moonstone Dragon

Chang gathered up pieces of wood around in the forest and made a fire with them. He was looking for food he could catch quickly and fix for his supper when Eel asked, "What about the preserved food in your sacks? You have loads. Why don't you eat some?"

Chang had forgotten all about the food he'd brought from home, but before he could head to the sacks, Eel called out, "Chang, come here and show me all the scars and bruises."

One by one, Chang revealed his battle wounds, and as he did, Eel stuck his tongue out and licked each one. Just like before, they had vanished without a single mark left on his body.

Chang thanked Eel then went to the sacks and found a few fish that were preserved in a jar and roasted them over the fire while Black Beauty grazed nearby. After Chang roasted the first fish, he took all the meat off and gave it the puppies, making sure that no bones were in the fish; he then roasted two more fish, gave one to Eel, and kept one for himself. He threw all the bones in the canyon where the dragon's corpse lay then took out fresh water, put it in bowls, and passed them out to everyone; afterward, he then washed the bowls. He placed his grass mat on the ground, placed his pillow on the mat, and slept with his blanket.

Everyone was asleep except for Eel. He never slept unless he was alone. Since he now had a family of dogs, a horse, and a human, he had to protect them with his life.

When morning arrived, Eel and Black Beauty were awake, and the puppies were playing. Chang put his sleeping equipment away, packed up Black Beauty, and took out the map. The picture of the Coral Dragon was gone, and there were only three dragons remaining. Chang looked at the bottom left dragon and saw it was the Moonstone Dragon. Before leaving, he examined the two pieces of the stone and the two gems then jumped on Black Beauty.

Eel inquired, "We are heading southeast, right?"

"Yes, we are," Chang said. "You lead the way and we will follow after you."

Eel headed out with Black Beauty right behind him. They ran and ran until night fell, but they still kept on running until morning arrived, and they stopped at a stream. Chang took out the map and saw that their location seemed safe enough. He jumped off Black Beauty and allowed them to rest while he collected fresh water, took out fresh clothes, and went for a dip in the stream. After drying off, he sat down next to Eel and asked, "How long have you been living in this forest?"

"Very long, in fact I can't explain how long I have been here," Eel shrugged.

"Do you think my master is proud of me for slaying those two dragons?" Chang ventured.

"Oh, yes, he is. I can assure you that he's full of joy and proud of you for killing those dragons and for retrieving the two pieces of the stone and the gems," Eel said.

"But I just took away a creature's life," Chang frowned.

"Yes, I know, but these creatures don't deserve to live,' Eel said.

"Well, that is a little bit harsh."

"I know, but you need to care about the ones you live with, and you need to care about your own life. Your life is more important," Eel explained.

"Oh," Chang said and went silent for a moment. "Well, I think we better get going," Chang said, starting to get up.

"Chang, what's the rush? You need to relax. We've been traveling the whole night and we need the rest," Eel insisted.

"Okay." Chang plopped back down.

It was peaceful, the sound of the stream, the chirping of birds, sun staring down onto the earth, the sounds of fish jumping in the water, and the view of beautiful flowers that blossomed all around. It was such a peaceful day that they didn't feel like doing anything at all until a huge rhinoceros appeared.

Chang hopped to his feet as did Eel, who asked, "What do you want?"

"I want you out of my territory!" the rhinoceros snapped.

"Since when did this part of the forest become your territory?" Eel challenged.

"Since the time I've lived here!" the rhinoceros snorted.

"You don't own this or any part of the forest. Animals are free to roam anywhere they please," Eel corrected him.

"Eel, I think we should just leave," Chang interjected in a whisper.

"Chang, shut up and stay out of this!" Eel scolded.

"Since you say so, why don't we battle to find out?" the Rhinoceros suggested.

"Yeah, let's battle," Eel agreed.

Chang took his sword out, and all three of them faced off. Eel did something that Chang had never seen before. He let lose with a huge roar that sent the rhinoceros to the other end of the forest. Chang was in such shock that he dropped his sword and his mouth plopped wide open.

Eel turned to him and said, "Chang, close your mouth or you'll catch crickets. They're healthy, but the ones here aren't very good-tasting."

Chang obeyed, but he was still staring at the same spot where the rhino had been. "Chang, is there something wrong?" Eel inquired.

"No," Chang replied.

"Then pick up your sword, we need to get going.

Chang grabbed his sword and put it away; he jumped on Black Beauty, took out the map, and saw there was a cave about seven hours away. He estimated, "Eel, we should be reaching a cave by nightfall."

Eel took off southeast, and Black Beauty followed after him. They ran and they ran until the late afternoon fell, but they didn't stop. When the sun disappeared over the horizon, there still was no cave. They halted and Eel said, "Chang, are you sure that we were supposed to reach the cave by nightfall?"

"Yes, I have never been wrong when it comes to traveling."

"Then, why don't I see a cave?' Eel asked, looking up at Chang.

"Well, maybe the map is wrong?" Chang offered.

"No magical map will ever be wrong or give us wrong directions, and that is a fact," Eel said, irritated with Chang. "Just give the map, now!"

Chang handed the map down to Eel, who took it with his mouth, put it on the ground, and held it down with his paws.

"The cave is another five hours away," Eel said, shooting Chang a hard look.

"Oh," Chang shrugged innocently.

"Well, now we have to run for another five hours. If you'd have measured more accurately, we could've been there by now!" Eel shouted at Chang.

Eel handed the map back and Chang said, "Well, when I looked at the map, the cave was there and not over here." Chang was pointing to the spot where he saw the cave was, then he pointed at the place where Eel said the cave was.

"Chang, stop! The cave is neither where you said it was nor neither where I said it was," Eel said mysteriously.

"What do you mean?" Chang was confused.

"Just look at the map," Eel said.

Chang surveyed the map and saw that Eel was right. "Eel, how can that be?"

"This cave has a dark force. On a normal map, it won't change because it wants to lure you into the trap, but on a magical map, it will warn you about the two places where the dark force is located," Eel told Chang.

"Oh, but I still want to check it out," Chang insisted.

"No! People say that they have been lured into this trap, and a horrible monster, the most hideous and the scariest monster, lives there. He does that to catch his prey," Eel cautioned.

"I still want to go," Chang demanded.

"I said no!" Eel shouted.

"I still want to go," Chang said in a scary manner.

"Oh no," Eel said, more to himself, "the dark force has set a spell on you. The only way to break it is to bite you."

Chang continued chanting the same sentence over and over again. When he got off the horse, Eel quickly pounced on him and bit him on the leg. Chang screamed, but the spell quickly wore off. Chang was still in pain, and Eel licked the bite mark so it would go away.

Chang shook it off then jumped back on his horse. They looked at the map and saw there was a river just another seven hours away from where they were.

Eel led the way, and Black Beauty followed after. They ran and ran until morning arrived, and they still ran until they reached the river they'd been wanting to get to. Chang jumped off Black Beauty, put the puppies on the ground, and removed everything from Black Beauty. They were all exhausted, the puppies had developed strong teeth, and were starting to get bigger. They were also starting to get rough, but they were still small enough to fit in the basket, but after five more days, they wouldn't be able to fit in the basket and would have to both start running. Chang gave everyone food and water; after, they all ate, he washed the bowls and collected fresh water. They all relaxed and Chang spoke up, "Eel, you still didn't tell me why you have a sea creature's name."

"That's because you must work it out for yourself." Eel flashed Chang a sly smile.

"Please, can you tell me, please, pretty please with crickets on top!" Chang pleaded.

Eel laughed and said, "My dear boy, you will have to work it out for yourself."

"But you always told me that, and you said you will tell me later, and later is now," Chang whimpered.

"Well, I lied," Eel chuckled.

"But you are like someone who never lies, but the first time you've just lied," Chang said, confused.

"Everyone lies, including spiritual people. They lie, too, Chang," Eel said. "Tell me, how many times have you lied?"

"I have never lied in my life…" Chang boasted.

Eel looked at him warily and Chang said, "Okay, maybe, no, I may have lied quite a lot."

"You see what I mean?" Eel said. "I have lied many times in my past life and in my life right now."

"Eel, I'm tired. I don't want to go anywhere today, I just want to sleep and relax," Chang said to change the subject.

"I know, literally, everyone is tired, the wolves, the horse, you and I are all extremely tired,'" Eel concurred.

"I'm going to sleep." Chang yawned.

"That is a good idea. You really need the shut-eye," Eel observed.

Chang took out his grass mat, his pillow, and his blanket; then he immediately passed out. Black Beauty and the wolves all slept, but not Eel; he stayed awake the whole morning.

When afternoon arrived, Chang went to sit by Eel and asked, "Can you tell me how old you are?"

"My dear boy, a magical creature like myself can never tell a mortal like yourself their true age, because a lot of mayhem can be created," Eel replied.

"What kind of mayhem will happen if you told me your true age?"

"You would never want to know. It is very ugly and cruel, and I don't want that to happen," Eel assured him.

"Eel, can these wolves talk now since they have gotten bigger?" Chang asked.

"Yes, they will soon talk. I think you should think about naming them because they need to respond to those names, just like Black Beauty and I."

"How about Ding and Dong?" Chang chirped.

"That's a great name. I'm sure that will be easy to remember, otherwise if you don't, you would be really daft," Eel snickered.

Chang let out a sarcastic laugh, turned to the side, closed his eyes, and muttered to himself, "Ding and Dong, Ding and Dong, Ding and Dong."

"Chang, shouldn't we get going?" Eel said, a little irritated.

"Just relax. I don't know where you are rushing off to." Chang shrugged.

"Well, the sooner we get to the Moonstone Dragon, the sooner we slay the dragon and get the stone and the gem," Eel said.

"Good point, but I still want to relax and I only want to leave tomorrow," Chang said firmly.

Chang was lying on the ground, looking at the sky wearing its orange and pink coat, and the trees shedding off old leaves; the beautiful flowers were closing to go to bed, but as soon as night fell, there was extreme silence. The only sound to be heard was that of crickets rubbing their feet together. Chang and Eel were the only ones awake; Chang continued looking up at the sky as did Eel, observing the moon and stars above them. Chang broke the silence. "Eel, the sky wears the most beautiful coat at night…the way the stars twinkle and the moon stares at me."

"Chang, those stars that sit in the sky are our ancestors looking at us," Eel said. "Do you see that big, shining star over there?" Eel pointed to the star with his paw.

"Yes."

"That star is your Master Lee looking down at you, but other people who look up at that star think it is the most important loved one they lost."

"Oh."

"You see, since Black Beauty lost her mother, she has feelings and also thinks that big star is her mother, and so do Ding and Dong."

"So we all think that our most loved one is that huge star?" Chang asked for confirmation.

"Yes."

"Eel, who is your most loved one that you lost?" Chang asked.

"It was my dear son, Ling. He was my only son, but those poachers from the land they call Europe killed my son for his teeth, skin, and meat," Eel said sadly.

"I'm sorry," Chang said softly.

"Don't be." Eel intimated.

"Oh," Chang said as another thought occurred to him. "Is the reason you don't want to tell me why your name is a sea creature's name also because mayhem will happen?"

"No, no, mayhem will not happen," Eel shook his head. "You should be able to find out for yourself. If you put the words in the right order you should be able figure out why I have that name. I still won't tell you, but I'll give you a hint…that phrase that keeps on ringing in your head."

"What about the phrase?" Chang asked.

Eel laughed. "I'm sure that you'll soon find out. Maybe after you retrieve the lost treasure of Shanghai you might figure it out." When the boy didn't reply, Eel said, "Chang, do you want to travel tonight so we can get closer to the Moonstone Dragon?"

"I think we should, we've had enough rest," Chang agreed.

"Okay," Eel nodded.

"Eel, why don't you ever sleep?" Chang asked.

"I don't sleep because of your safety. I have to guard your horse, your wolves, and you with my life. You all mean a lot to me, and I don't want to lose you like I lost my son."

"But don't you ever get sleepy, and don't your eyes pain because you're keeping your eyes are open all day and all night?" Chang inquired.

"Sometimes, but I have this power that gives me energy," Eel told Chang.

"Eel, will Ding and Dong be able to run as fast as you when we are traveling?" Chang brightened.

"Yes, they will. They could even overtake me because they are young and I am old, but they won't overtake us because they don't know the route to where we are going. They will be able to pick up a few scents, but your journey in the forest is nearly over and you will have to go back to the village. Don't think that after you slay all the dragons your adventure is done. You will then have to get into the chamber, get into the palace, and put everything in order."

"Eel, I don't mean to put you off or anything, but right now, we need to do more traveling and less talking, we can talk along the way," Chang teased.

"You're the one who is asking so many questions," Eel muttered.

"What was that?" Chang asked briskly.

"Nothing."

They packed all their things; Eel, Ding and Dong were all standing beside Black Beauty. Chang took out the map and looked at the Moonstone Dragon and saw they were only three days away. He looked for a place where they could camp and saw there was a field full of fruits and vegetables. Chang showed Eel the map pointing to the location of the field, and fortunately it was not a dark force.

Chang estimated. "Eel, the distance from here to that field is approximately eighty hours away. We should reach there in the early hours of the morning."

"The moon will guide us there and so will the stars at this time," Eel said.

"Eel, you lead the way. Ding and Dong will follow, and then we'll follow on after them." Chang indicated himself and Black Beauty.

Eel nodded his head. They ran in the silent night. Sounds of the crickets were not to be heard; the only noise was the sound of hooves and paws running. The early hours of the morning arrived, the sky's beautiful coat of stars and a moon had disappeared. The sky now wore its yellow and orange coat. Up ahead, they could see a field; they continued walking, and when they arrived, half of the field was full of food, and the other half was just plain. This place was perfect to camp; plus they had scored themselves some breakfast. Actually, Chang realized, the only creatures who scored breakfast were himself and Black Beauty because they were able to eat all of those things. But Eel, Ding, and Dong struck out because they were carnivores.

Chang spotted two white rabbits and unsheathed his sword, but Eel stopped him, saying, "Don't kill those poor, innocent creatures to feed us. Magical animals eat everything and anything including fruit and vegetables."

"In that case, everyone's scored breakfast," Chang said happily then collected wood for a fire. Chang cooked vegetables for everyone.

After breakfast, he washed the bowls and put them away, and later he found a small watering hole; everything was just perfect. But did anyone live here? If anyone did, they would have been eating their food, and sure enough, an ox emerged from behind a bush and made its way toward them, asking, "Who are you?"

"I am Chang, the apprentice of the late Master Lee. These are my wolf pets, Ding and Dong; this is my pet tiger, Eel; and this is my pet horse, Black Beauty," Chang introduced them.

"My name is Shirley," the ox said.

"Shirley, we don't mean to trespass on your territory, we were just hungry and tired, and we needed a place to camp for the night. I hope you don't mind us being here," Chang said tentatively.

Oh, I don't mind. It's an extreme pleasure to have you. Chang, you, and your wonderful pets are welcome to stay on my territory. It has been ages since anyone has come here, and I will treat you like family for this one night—and don't worry, this place is very safe, and we can all have a peaceful night's sleep," Shirley assured them.

"Thank you, Shirley. Your hospitality is appreciated," Chang bowed.

"You're welcome. Make yourselves at home."

"Thank you once again." Chang had an afterthought.

"Shirley, how did ever get these vegetables to grow when you don't have any hands?"

"Well, Chang"—Shirley smiled—"all the creatures in the forest are magical...except for some that come from foreign lands, like that horse of yours. Well, it is the grace of the magical spirits and our ancestors to help us get food."

"Shirley, Eel never sleeps and he says that he never gets tired," Chang tossed out.

"He is doing it for your safety. Magical creatures also get tired, but we have a power that will allow us to boost our energy up," Shirley explained.

"Oh."

A little later, Chang reclined on his back looking at the sky wearing its solid blue coat; nothing could ruin this beautiful day. Everyone was relaxing and having fun; Ding and Dong were playing, Black Beauty was drinking water from the watering hole, Eel was sleeping for the first time, and Shirley was eating grass and Chang was enjoying the sky. The only sounds to be heard were the birds chirping. Everything was so beautiful, rabbits were scattered all around, butterflies fluttered everywhere, and birds continued to chirp the whole day.

When the late afternoon arrived, Eel awoke from his slumber, and everyone was still relaxing. Eel was drinking so much water it looked like he was dehydrated and his face looked so fierce.

Eel came back and lay down on the grass and was not talking at all. Finally, Chang asked, "Eel, what is the matter?"

"Nothing, I was just thinking about the dream I had while I was sleeping,"

"What did you dream about?"

"I will tell you tomorrow," Eel put him off. "Why don't you go collect some food and cook it so we can eat?" Chang got up and collected vegetables from the garden and cooked them. Everyone ate then fell right to sleep, except for Eel.

When morning arrived, everyone was awake, everything was packed and tied to Black Beauty; Chang collected fresh water and fresh fruits and vegetables. He took out the map and looked at the Moonstone Dragon, estimating they were ten hours away. Chang jumped on Black Beauty and said farewell to Shirley. Eel led the way, Ding and Dong followed, and Black Beauty followed after them. They ran and ran until late afternoon when they arrived at a beach surrounding a lake. Chang hid Black Beauty and Ding and Dong in case the dragon arrived.

Before leaving them, Chang explained everything to Ding and Dong, and to his surprise, they answered with "yes." He left them and went back to the beach. Chang put out his grass mat next to Eel and lay on the sand. Night had fallen; Chang was still awake, star gazing. Chang was only looking at the big star even though all the other stars were twinkling brightly.

"Are they trying to warn us of something?" Chang wondered aloud.

"Who knows?" Eel replied.

But the night was so peaceful and Chang and Eel wanted to go back to Black Beauty and Ding and Dong. Apparently the dragon wasn't coming. The full moon had emerged from behind the dark clouds, and Ding and Dong howled. When the reflection of the moon was clear in the water, bubbles started to come up. Chang and Eel both jumped up. Chang grabbed his sword. The bubbles were there for a minute, and then a huge dragon emerged from the water; it was the Moonstone Dragon, and the armor from head to tail stood out.

The Moonstone Dragon bellowed, "Who dares to enter my territory?"

"I am Chang, the apprentice of the late Master Lee, and this is my pet, Eel," Chang spoke confidently.

"You have no right to enter my territory. Only the ones that are worthy to me may enter—but you are not worthy to me. You are of no use to me and neither is your pet," the Moonstone Dragon proclaimed.

"Well, you are not worthy to me either, but you are of use to me and you don't even deserve to live," Chang spat back.

"Oh yeah? Well neither do you," the Moonstone Dragon huffed. "You deserve to die right in front of my face, right here and right now."

"Then what are we waiting for?" Chang spun his sword for one revolution.

"Yes, then what are we waiting for?" the Moonstone Dragon mocked then blew white flames into the air, setting the palm trees on the beach afire.

The Moonstone Dragon was still in the lake; he rocketed out of the water and hit Eel with his huge tail. Eel rolled over and over then got back to his feet and let out his huge roar. The dragon fell back into the lake and instantly rose up again.

Chang ran toward the lake and Eel shouted, "Chang, what are you doing?!"

"Something I should have done a long time ago!" Chang shouted back, diving into the water with his sword. He swam right to the bottom where the dragon's legs and stomach were exposed. But before he could stab the dragon, a hammerhead shark appeared. *Uh-oh, didn't figure on that*, Chang thought and quickly swam to the surface. But the shark got hold of his leg and dragged him back down toward the bottom. Chang stabbed the shark with his sword, but it didn't let go of his leg. It continued to drag him downward. When they reached the bottom, Chang was running out of breath and frantically tried to pry open the shark's jaws. The shark was dying from loss of blood and could no longer hold on. Chang succeeded in opening the shark's jaws and swam to the surface to take a breath.

Chang broke the surface, gasped for air, and saw that Eel and the Moonstone Dragon were still engaged in combat.

When Eel had spotted Chang, he shouted, "Chang, hurry up and attack the weak spots that are under the water!"

"Sorry, I was…" Chang started to say.

"No chatting, hurry!" Eel shouted.

Chang dove back in the water with the sword clenched in his teeth. He swam to the bottom to where the dragon's legs and stomach were vulnerable to attack. But just then, another hammerhead shark was darting toward him.

Chang thought, *I have no time for this!* He brandished the sword, made an angry face, and scared the shark away. He swam to the bottom and stabbed the legs of the dragon and then the stomach.

Eel jumped on the dragon and used his teeth to bite the dragon's neck. Just before the dragon went down, Eel used his teeth to get the gem out and quickly jumped off when the dragon sunk back in the water.

At the same time, Chang was swimming to the surface. The dragon got hold of Chang's foot and dragged him down with him. Chang was again running out of oxygen and needed to get to the surface for fresh air, or he would drown.

When Eel looked down in the water and saw Chang's predicament, he dove in and swam to the bottom to help. Eel needed every bit of strength he had left to pry open the jaws of the dragon, and Chang frantically swam to the surface. But Chang had forgotten to get the stone from around the dragon's neck.

Fortunately, Eel noticed this, and with his last ounce of energy, he ripped the stone from around the dragon's neck and kicked his legs for the surface. Chang and Eel's heads came out of the water at the same time. They helped each other swim to the shore, both exhausted, but worst of all, Chang was in extreme pain because of the shark bite on his leg. The moonstone gem lay on the sand. Chang grabbed it and put it in his pocket. Eel put the stone down and shook his body to get rid of excess water; Chang followed suit and shook his head to get rid of any water, and right after that, Eel's fur poofed up into a bush.

Chang burst out laughing. "You...you look like something just exploded in your fur."

"Ha ha," Eel said sarcastically. He noticed that Chang's hair also looked like something exploded in it. Eel doubled over with laughter and said, "Now that's what I call funny!"

"Hey, at least it is only on my head and not all over, and I don't look like a bush baby," Chang taunted.

"Your hair looks like a porcupine," Eel snickered.

"I'm in such pain," Chang said between giggles. "But all this laughing about hair made me forget about the shark bite." He then became quite serious. "What if I bleed to death and then I don't complete this journey?"

"Chang, relax. You're not going to bleed to death as long as I am here," Eel chortled.

"M-maybe the M-moonstone D-Dragon was right? M-maybe I wasn't going to d-die right in front of him, b-but I am d-dying right h-here!?" Chang babbled, watching his blood ooze out of his leg, showing no signs of stopping.

"Chang, relax, I will heal it now, just relax," Eel said calmly.

Chang sat on the grass, still panicking, while Eel dipped his paw in water and placed it over Chang's bite. Moments later, the bite was gone, and Chang was in no more pain.

Eel said smugly, "Now, do you still going to think that you are going to die here?'"

"No." Chang blushed with embarrassment.

"As long as I am here, nothing will go wrong," Eel said.

Eel carried Chang's grass mat and Chang carried the gem and stone back to the place where they had hid Black Beauty and Ding and Dong, all the while thinking, *But what happens if for some reason Eel's not here?*

The Sapphire Dragon

When they arrived to where they'd had hid Black Beauty and Ding and Dong, Chang didn't eat. Once everyone was asleep except for Eel, he took out the pieces of the stone and put them in place. He just needed two more pieces to complete the stone, and then they could go to the chamber that was underneath the palace that no one knew about. He put the pieces away and took out the map and saw that the Moonstone Dragon was no longer there; the only two dragons left on the map were the Sapphire Dragon and the Diamond Dragon. His journey in the forest was almost coming to an end, but then again, you never know what lies in the chamber.

Chang put the map away and lay down and asked Eel, "Can you remember the last time you saw your son?"

"The last time I saw him was the time they took him away from me," Eel said, his face forlorn.

"Then how did you know that he was killed by the poachers?"

"Like I told you before, Chang, I know everything that happens in this forest, I can sense everything and anything," Eel said.

"But it didn't happen in the forest," Chang corrected him.

"Chang, I didn't tell you that it didn't happen in the forest. I didn't even tell where they were."

"I know," Chang said.

"Then why did you say it?"

"I felt like it," Chang shrugged.

"But this all happened in the forest, they also tried to capture me, but they said I was too old and I was not worth it," Eel sneered.

"You understand what they said?" Chang said, surprised.

"I know every language, I understand every language, and I can speak every language," Eel said matter-of-factly.

"So you understand the language of the Europeans?" Chang asked.

"Didn't you hear what I said? I said…"

"I heard what you said," Chang broke in. "I was just in shock."

"In shock of what?"

"I mean, even the people who stay here that come from foreign lands don't understand every single language," Chang offered.

"Chang, it is hard to understand and speak every language," Eel said.

"But you are an animal. You've never been exposed to any of these languages or heard of these languages," Chang said in wonderment.

"Well, I am a magical animal, and I live in a magical forest. Any language that anyone speaks sounds like English to me, but in a different form," Eel explained.

"I am going to sleep." Chang shook his tired head.

Chang fell asleep, but Eel remained awake the whole night. The night was soundless except for the buzzing of the blood thirsty mosquitos.

Eel looked up and saw a shooting star go by. He said his wish aloud: "I wish that Chang will retrieve the lost treasure of Shanghai without any troubles."

After Eel said his wish, all the stars twinkled nonstop, and a smile had appeared on Chang's face. Eel then heard something walking in the forest. He got up and scanned the area, and when his eyes passed a tree, Eel thought he saw something. He returned his gaze to the same spot, and there was a saber-toothed tiger. Eel walked up to the tiger and asked, "Who are you?"

"I am Emma. I come from the snowy parts of the forest," she said evenly.

"I am Eel. I live with my family...a horse, two wolves, and a human."

"Human, eh?" Emma said, smacking her lips. "Horse, too?"

"Yeah, why?" Eel said suspiciously.

"Well, maybe they could be a tasty snack?" Emma said, grinning from ear to ear.

Eel pounced on Emma, and she flung him off her. Eel rolled once then came up on all fours. They slowly walked in a circle, and finally, Emma said, "Feisty, you are."

"Why don't you meet your destiny of death?" Eel sneered.

"Well, maybe you will also be a delectable meal?" Emma ran her tongue along her six-inch canines.

Emma broke into a run toward him, but Eel roared and slammed his paws to the ground. The earth beneath them shook. Emma stopped, let out a roar, and lightning and thunder filled the sky.

A pack of saber-toothed tigers emerged out of trees and bushes. Eel roared and first Chang, then Black Beauty and Ding and Dong all magically disappeared.

Emma took it all in stride. "Hope you don't mind, my brothers and sisters feel a bit hungry, too, and since the appetizers are no longer there, we're afraid we'll have to eat you instead. Your own kind is eating you, and it's a shame, poor you, but that's how life is, isn't it? Kill him!" Emma commanded the others.

All the saber-toothed tigers, including Emma, leapt into the air. They all piled on top of Eel. He roared even louder than last time, and all the saber-toothed tigers flew off of him. Eel's claws instantly grew longer, and his teeth became bigger and sharper. In lightning-fast motion, Eel attacked and killed all the saber-toothed tigers—except for Emma.

"I see you have killed all my brothers and sisters, but you have not killed me," Emma observed.

"Well, you better say good-bye because I may be the last creature you ever see in your life," Eel snorted.

"Like I said before, you are a feisty old man," Emma acknowledged.

"Well, I am going to get even feistier," Eel said.

"Roar like a dinosaur," Emma challenged him.

Eel jumped onto Emma, and she spat, "I didn't say pounce like a pansy, I said roar like a dinosaur."

"I don't like sarcasm," Eel roared then killed Emma, and that was the last sound that Emma heard and the last creature she ever saw in her life.

Eel's paws and mouth were full of blood. He roared for a short rain and washed himself off. He then roared again and Chang, Black Beauty and Ding and Dong reappeared. He lay down by Chang and licked his paws, for they were very sore. Eel was now very tired and wanted to sleep, but he had to stay awake in case anything else came by while he was asleep.

When morning arrived, everyone was wide awake, but Eel asked, "Chang, can we leave in the afternoon? I am extremely tired."

"Of course..." Chang looked at his weary friend. "What happened?"

"Well, while you were sleeping, Emma, a saber-toothed tiger, came here along with her brothers and sisters, looking to have you for their supper. But I made you disappear, so they tried to kill me—but I took care of them..." he winked with much effort. "Then I brought you back and now I'm exhausted."

"Wow, some night you had." Chang patted his friend on the shoulder. "Since you say that, where's Emma?"

Eel slowly got up and led Chang to where Emma was. Eel had hidden Emma behind a bush. He explained how her brothers and sisters had disappeared.

"I've never seen a saber-toothed tiger before," Chang marveled. "But I have heard of them. I would like to take its tooth for a souvenir."

"Chang, you can't take the tooth," Eel said, blocking him. "This is a magical creature, and since her own kind killed her, you can't touch her…only her kind. If you do, you will be gone."

"What do you mean by 'gone'?" Chang pressed.

"I mean you will go bye-bye, birdie," Eel said.

"But I don't want to go bye-bye, birdie." Chang made a scared face. "I need to retrieve the lost treasure of Shanghai."

"Exactly. Now please, can I go sleep?" Eel pleaded.

"Then go sleep. Who asked you to start talking?" Chang smirked.

"You are the one who started asking me," Eel growled.

"Oh yes. Good night, sleep tight, and don't let the saber-toothed tigers bite." Chang laughed and said to himself, "I kill me."

"Ha-ha. Yes, you kill everyone," Eel said sarcastically.

Eel went and slept while Chang was busy talking to Ding and Dong and teaching them how to kill. The morning went by quickly, then the afternoon. Eel was still sleeping when evening fell, and he didn't wake up until the wee hours of the next morning.

Chang woke up too and said, "You told me you were going to sleep until the afternoon, but you didn't get up. When evening came, you still didn't get up. We have been in this place for three days because it is now just before dawn!" Chang snapped.

"Calm down," Eel said through a yawn. "You are not the one who fought a bunch of saber-toothed tigers. You are not the one staying up the whole night guarding in case any danger comes."

Chang relaxed and said, "We will leave as soon as the sun rises."

"Fine," Eel agreed.

Eel went back to sleep and so did Chang. When the sun had risen, they packed all their things and Chang took out the map. "Eel, we will have to travel southwest to get to the Sapphire Dragon."

"Okay, but how many days away?" Eel asked.

"It is five days," Chang said.

"Do Ding and Dong understand you?" Eel asked.

"Yes, they do understand me, and they can also talk too," Chang said.

"Is it the same that I lead the way, Ding and Dong follow me, and then you follow on after them?" Eel asked.

"Yes," Chang said then became pensive. "Eel, do you think that we will get to the chamber and retrieve the lost treasure of Shanghai?"

"Chang, do I look like a fortune teller?" Eel snickered. "We shall see what we shall see."

"Okay," Chang shrugged.

"Can we go now?" Eel indicated the trail with his head.

"Yes," Chang said, perturbed that Eel might be keeping something from him.

Eel headed southwest, Ding and Dong followed, and Chang took the rear. They ran and ran without stopping, having wasted a whole day yesterday not traveling. When it was late afternoon, they were still running, and when evening arrived, they were still running without stopping; not until the next morning did they stop. Black Beauty was exhausted, and they rested next to a pond. Chang took a dip, came out, and put a fresh set of clothes on.

Chang sat down on his grass mat. He was tired but not hungry. It was then that Master Lee came to his mind and those words kept on ringing in his head nonstop.

Eel observed him for a moment then asked, "Is there something wrong, Chang?"

"No, I was just thinking about Master Lee and those words."

"Chang, your master will forever remain in your memory, and those words that keep on ringing in your head too will forever remain in your mind."

"Eel, you always have a way with words to comfort me," Chang smiled.

"I know." Eel hesitated then said, "Chang?"

"Mmm… I'm listening." Chang had a dreamy look in his eyes.

"Don't forget that your master will be here and here…" Eel put his paw by Chang's heart and head.

"I know." Chang nodded.

"Did you ever find out why my name is a sea creature's name?" Eel asked to cheer him up.

"Not really," Chang said looking at Eel.

"Then why don't you give it try and guess?" Eel suggested.

"I think I will, let me see…mmmmm…" Chang scrunched his face up with the effort. "I can't really say, but I think Eel?"

"No, but can you guess anything other than that?"

"No."

"Maybe some other time you can get it right?"

"Yeah, maybe."

"But tell me, didn't you learn anything about that big star I told you about?"

"I did. It's just that I feel that you are Master Lee just sitting there, but in a different form," Chang said in frustration.

"Chang, now do you know who I am?" Eel asked with a smile on his face.

"What do you mean?" Chang turned to Eel.

"You actually got my real name!" Eel exclaimed.

"You mean, Eel?" Chang said, looking confused.

"No, the other name," Eel said anxiously.

"You mean, Lee?" Chang said, looking more confused.

"If you spell Lee backward, you get…" Eel prompted.

"It spells Eel, so?" Chang threw up his hands.

"If you spell Eel backward, you get…"

"It spells Lee…" Chang's eyes got bigger. "You mean that you are the reincarnation of Master Lee?"

Eel nodded his head and smiled. "Yes, it is I you see. I have told you that I will be with you every step you take."

"Wow! It is you, but you are different," Chang exclaimed.

"He saw that you needed me the most, so he sent me down as a tiger to help you complete your journey."

"You see, you are not the only one living the dream to go on such a great adventure, we both are."

Chang sat there the whole day. It was truly shocking to find out a tiger that he'd found in the forest was actually his Master Lee in a different form, and luckily, he took this tiger in; otherwise he wouldn't have had his master by his side and that would have been a disaster. When night fell, Chang was still sitting in the same position thinking about the same thing over and over again nonstop until Lee said, "Chang, can we go now?"

"Where?" Chang shook himself out of his reverie. "Oh, traveling, yes, we need to pack so we can get going."

"Okay, I will wake Black Beauty and Ding and Dong," Eel said.

"Okay, you do that," Chang said with no interest while packing his things away in the supply sacks.

Lee roared and Black Beauty and Ding Dong awakened with shock. Chang scanned the area in case he forgot anything then jumped on Black Beauty.

They ran and ran for the whole night. Not until the following night did they stop for a rest. They were exhausted, but they made a fire and ate.

Black Beauty was fast asleep, but not Lee, Chang, and Ding and Dong. For the first time did they talk at length and Ding said, "Chang, is this tiger really your master?"

"Yes, he was, but he then died and came in the form of a tiger," Chang explained.

"Oh," Ding and Dong said.

"Chang, you don't expect them to understand what you just said?" Lee asked.

"Yes," Chang said matter-of-factly.

"Even though they can talk, they are still young and still need to learn. Sure they understood what you said when we were going to slay the Moonstone Dragon, but that they understood because they have been with you so long, and they saw you slay your first dragon, and so did I," Lee said.

"You mean you were following me?" Chang said, surprised.

"Yes, because I needed to keep track of where you were."

"Can you smell me or sniff me out?" Chang asked.

"Yes, if I have known the smell for a long time, but you, I forget your scent so I had to follow you. But don't forget I am still old...I'm one hundred years old, and you are seventeen years old. If you were me, you could have remembered every single scent, but it's not so easy when you're old," Lee acknowledged.

"So those words were true...you were going to stick with me every step I took," Chang said then narrowed his eyes.

"But you weren't when I was slaying the Emerald Dragon."

"Yes, I was. You just didn't see me," Lee said. "But remember this, Chang, I will be with you no matter what happens, I will be with you through everything," Lee said.

"I kind of miss the old you. You're now a magical tiger who has the voice of my master, but it is kind of hard looking at you in the body of a tiger," Chang admitted.

"Chang, I could have come in any form. I could have come in the form of one the wolves. But I chose the form of a tiger for you to be brave and stay with animals that come from this forest where humans don't want to come. You came into this forest with courage and the guts to try to slay all five dragons."

"I know," Chang said. "But the Diamond Dragon is double the size of each dragon."

"Well, you're going to have a lot of help. Ding and Dong will help, and so will I," Lee said. "No matter what happens, even if I have to risk my life to save your life, I will do it." Lee pledged.

"So will I," Ding and Dong said at the same time.

"And I am also sure Black Beauty would do the same," Lee said.

"I would risk my life for any of you guys just to save yours, and that is a fact," Chang affirmed.

"Ding and Dong, you go to bed," Lee ordered.

"We don't want to, we're not tired at all," Ding said, and Dong nodded his head.

"Don't make me get the fuzzy tiger to tickle you all the way to tickle land," Lee threatened good-naturedly.

Ding and Dong went to bed because the fuzzy tiger that would tickle them all the way to tickle land was in fact Lee. Lee loved children and animals.

Lee came and sat down by Chang and said, "Please give me the map."

"Okay," Chang said, handing it over.

Lee held the map down with his paws so the map wouldn't fly away; they were very close to the Sapphire Dragon. "Chang, why don't you clean that sword of yours. You need to always have a clean sword when you going to fight something."

"But," Chang objected, "my sword *is* clean!"

"What about the handle?" Lee challenged him.

"It's clean," Chang declared.

"Your sword is covered in beach sand," Lee pointed at it with his nose.

Chang got up and cleaned his sword then came back to sit back by Lee, who said, "Why don't you go to sleep?"

"But…" Chang started to say.

"But? No buts. You need the rest and don't let me have to get the fuzzy tiger for you." Lee raised an eyebrow.

"Please," Chang scoffed, "there is no such thing as a fuzzy tiger."

"Oh really?" Lee moved quickly and tickled Chang unmercifully.

Chang burst into uncontrollable laughter. After a minute, Lee stopped and asked Chang, "Now do you believe there is such thing as a fuzzy tiger?"

"Now I do," Chang managed, gasping for breath.

"Now, you go to be, because I know you don't want another visit from the tickling fuzzy tiger?" Lee warned him.

"I'm going right to sleep, Master," Chang agreed.

"Good night, don't let the saber-toothed tigers bite," Lee quipped, imitating Chang.

"I'll make sure they bite you," Chang retorted.

Chang lay on his grass mat and drifted off to sleep. Lee remained awake and whispered into Chang's ear, "You better be ready for the Sapphire Dragon."

And with that, Lee put his head on his paws and watched everyone sleep.

When morning arrived, everything was packed away and tied to Black Beauty. Chang took the map out and determined they were fifty-four hours away from the Sapphire Dragon. *And the Sapphire Dragon is fifty-four hours away from death*, Chang confidently thought. He saw another place where they could camp and told Lee, "Master, there is a cave that is not far away, and you have to lead us there as always."

Lee nodded his head, and Chang put the map away and jumped on Black Beauty.

Lee started to run, Ding and Dong followed, and Black Beauty followed after them. Chang had many questions that he wanted to ask his master. Since the time his human master had died, he couldn't ask anyone. But now his human master came in the reincarnation of a talking tiger. He wanted to ask about the painting on the wall in the cave that his master had drawn. He wanted to know why his master never told him that he had owned a horse. How long had Master Lee been following him around? He had more questions than you can imagine since the time his human master died.

They came to a halt, and Chang came out of his daydreaming. There was a huge ditch that prevented them from continuing on. They couldn't go around it because it appeared to go on and on forever.

Chang called out, "Master Lee, how can we cross this ditch?"

"Ding, Dong, and I can jump this ditch, but Black Beauty can't and neither can you," Lee replied.

Chang didn't believe this to be so. "Black Beauty can take a long run up and jump this ditch. I'm sure she will make it, she has long legs."

"Chang, if she is going to try and jump this ditch, you can't be riding her, or both of you will die," Lee cautioned.

"Don't be too sure about that," Chang boasted. "Black Beauty and I will do it."

"Chang, I am telling you, it is a bad idea." Lee's warning was more firm this time.

But Chang was already backing a far distance for Black Beauty to take her long run up when he said, "Trust me, I know what I am doing."

Chang jumped on Black Beauty. She scraped the ground with her hooves, neighed, then broke into a run. She was running faster than lightning when she sped past Lee, Ding, and Dong, and leapt and soared through the air, set her front legs out…and she made it!

Lee was amazed, and so were Ding and Dong.

"I told you we were going to make it," Chang said, patting Black Beauty's neck with a big grin on his face.

"Don't rub it in." Lee shook his head in wonderment.

"Wow! That was amazing!" Ding exclaimed.

"Lee, is it our turn to jump over this big hole?" Dong asked.

"Yes, it is," Lee said.

Ding and Dong leapt from where they were. They soared magically over to the other side with plenty of room to spare, and so did Lee.

Chang pulled out the map and saw their destination; there was no ditch on the map until it had appeared.

He located his finger on the cave and said, "Lee, we will reach the cave by the late afternoon. We're only seven hours away, so the sooner we leave, the sooner we get there."

They all ran, and as soon as late afternoon arrived, there was the cave. They came to halt and Lee said, "Chang, Ding, Dong, and I will go and make sure there is nothing in the cave. You stay here."

"Okay." Chang nodded.

Lee, Ding, and Dong went into cave, and a minute later, they came out screaming and didn't stop until they were safely hidden behind Black Beauty. A huge grizzly bear sauntered out the cave, yelling, "And stay out! I don't want to see your furry butts ever in this cave again!"

"Now what do we do?" Chang frowned.

"Check the map and see if there is another destination not too far from here," Lee suggested.

Chang looked at the map and shook his head. "Lee, the nearest rest spot from here is a spring...but it is near the Sapphire Dragon."

"That can't be," Lee said in consternation. "Just hold the map so I can see it."

Chang held the map in position for Lee.

Lee had to agree. "Looks like we won't have any rest until tomorrow in the late afternoon, but I am sure we can rest here for an hour."

"Can't we at least travel for another two hours?" Chang suggested.

"Sorry, Chang, I am afraid we can't. Ding and Dong are tired," Lee said.

"I'm tired, too, but you don't see me complaining," Chang huffed.

"Chang, they are still small."

"So?" Chang argued.

"So they need to rest, otherwise when we are running, they will collapse because of lack of energy," Lee explained.

"We're tired," Ding and Dong whimpered and collapsed to the ground.

"Now do you see what I mean?" Lee tossed his head at the pups.

"Yes," Chang sighed.

"So are we camping here tonight?" Lee asked.

"Yes," Chang sighed louder.

Chang lay on his grass mat and looked up at the sky's coat of stars. He searched for the big star, and there it was. He said to himself, "Big star, you don't mean anything to me now since I have my master right here beside me."

"Chang," Lee spoke up, "I may live for eternity, but remember one thing, a human can't kill me, but my own kind can."

"Even the ones who are not from this forest?"

"Yes," Lee replied.

"But can other animals kill you?"

"No, only my kind, only tigers can kill me," Lee confirmed.

"Master Lee, since the time you have died, I have had many questions to ask but no one to tell them to," Chang ventured.

"I know that you had many questions to ask since the time I died. Now that I am here, you can ask me all the questions that you wanted to ask me," Lee said.

"That painting on the wall in the cave that I stayed in one of the nights when I was going to slay the Emerald Dragon, I saw the five dragons on the wall, all in the shape of a diamond, and all the four dragons were the same size and the Diamond Dragon was double the size of all of them. Even on the map it is the biggest dragon, but why?" Chang asked.

"Well, the answer to that is the Diamond Dragon is the eldest of the dragons, and the Emerald Dragon is the youngest out of them, and they are all brothers, and he can sense who you are," Lee replied. "Chang, you need to focus on the Sapphire Dragon and stop jumping ahead to the Diamond Dragon and going to the chamber and getting into the palace. That can all wait. First, you need to slay one dragon at a time, and then we can talk about that."

"I know, but I mean, we have a lot of things to do, but I just want to go home," Chang whined.

"Now that is not the young boy who craved for many adventures and used to climb trees and begged me to teach him the martial arts. I thought you wanted to go on this adventure because you found it fascinating and exciting and…and dangerous," Lee reproached him.

"I know, but I'm homesick…I just want to go home," Chang cried.

"Well, tell me, would it make your master proud of you to watch you give up?" Lee got all into Chang's face. "People who give up are fat warthogs and losers, and I know that you are not one of them, you are as fit as a cheetah. You can't just stop halfway and say that you don't want to slay anymore dragons and retrieve the lost treasure of Shanghai. I thought you really wanted to retrieve the lost treasure?"

"I do!" Chang exclaimed.

"Then why were you telling me you don't want to do it?"

"Who said I was?" Chang perked up.

"That's my boy," Lee smiled.

At that moment, Chang saw a shooting star and wished to be able to slay the Diamond dragon with ease.

Lee asked, "What did you wish for?"

"I can't tell you, my lips are sealed, and word of it will never come out." Chang pinched his lips together tightly.

"Thought as much." Lee smiled. "Go to bed because tomorrow we are reaching her."

"What do you mean her?"

"Never mind," Lee said cryptically. "Just go to bed."

Chang turned on his side and was wondering what his master meant by "we are reaching *her*." He kept thinking about it until he fell asleep. When morning arrived, everyone was awake, and they all needed to get going.

Chang got out the map and saw that they were two hours away from the Sapphire Dragon. He put the map away and jumped on Black Beauty. They ran southwest, and when two hours had passed, they found themselves in the snowy part of the forest. Chang dismounted Black Beauty, and as they walked together, they then saw a huge mountain with blue flames coming out from the top. They knew the dragon was high up on that mountain.

They continued walking through the snow, and a huge snake approached them. Black Beauty was neighing with fright and bolted from the path and into the forest. Ding and Dong followed Black Beauty to the forest to see where she was going. Chang and Lee were left alone, and the only weapons they had were a sword and Lee's sharp teeth and claws. But how were they going to kill this snake?

"What now?" Chang shivered.

"Chang, we have to get the flute of death to kill this snake…that is the only thing that will do the trick," Lee said without moving.

"How are we going kill it? Since while we are playing it, are we also going to die?" Chang said out of the side of his mouth.

"Don't worry about that," Lee said in a loud whisper.

"But where am I supposed to find it?" Chang asked.

Lee used his head to point Chang in the right direction, then dashed toward, and it attacked while Lee tried to distract him. This was Chang's time to go find the flute of death.

Chang ran far from Lee and was looking around the base of the mountain when he saw the flute. But it was frozen in ice, and Chang couldn't pry it out. Chang tried using his sword to break the ice, but it still wouldn't budge. With all his might, he stabbed the block and it started to crack, and then it broke and shattered into pieces. Chang got cut by a sharp sliver of ice, but he grabbed the flute and now needed to get back soon to Lee so he could kill the snake.

Chang huffed and puffed at full speed, all the way to Lee. Out of the corner of his eye, Lee spotted Chang and directed him where to go with a head motion. Chang hurried to position himself behind Lee without the snake noticing him.

Lee whispered, "Ready?"

"Ready," Chang whispered back.

Lee roared so loudly that it had made both of them temporarily deaf as Chang began playing the flute. The snake became highly agitated and lost control of itself and fell down to the ground with a huge *thud*, gasping its last few breaths before it died.

Lee roared softly, and their hearing magically returned. "That should do it," he proclaimed.

"Let's get going and slay the Sapphire Dragon before it gets too late," Chang said.

They both ran till they reached the mountain. Chang got there first and started to climb. It was very steep, and he yelled back to Lee, "There's got to be an easier way."

Lee roared, and both him and Chang disappeared from where they were and reappeared on top of the mountain. Lo and behold, there lay the majestic beast in all her glory and splendor, the Sapphire Dragon.

This will be easy, Chang thought, since the dragon was sleeping. But he was wrong. The dragon suddenly raised her head and cried, "Why do you awaken me from my slumber?"

"I am Lee, and this is Chang," Lee introduced them.

"I hate it when creatures awaken me from my slumber," she said crankily. "Everyone deserves to die except for us dragons. We deserve to live. We are the true rulers of Shanghai and the whole of China."

"No, you are not!" Chang shouted.

The Sapphire Dragon was furious and let out huge blue flames that engulfed Chang and Lee. They fell to ground from the smoke intoxication, but Chang was able to crawl on hands and knees through the smoke and get near the Sapphire Dragon.

When the smoke cleared the Sapphire Dragon was attacking Lee. Chang stabbed her stomach numerous times, but she didn't screech with pain.

Maybe she's a very powerful dragon? Chang wondered. He climbed onto her back and stabbed her from behind. Only then did she screech with pain and flail her body wildly back and forth. Chang climbed her neck and stabbed her head. And just like the snake, she then fell to the ground with a *thud*!

Lee ripped the stone from her neck and Chang used his sword to take the gem out. Chang jumped off the corpse and a ray of blue light shone from the clouds and set the Sapphire Dragon alight in blue flames. Chang and Lee watched her burn, and in the next moment, the mountain began to collapse in on itself.

Chang and Lee tried to get off, but it was too late. The mountain had already crumbled to the ground. Chang and Lee were under the rubble. Black Beauty and Ding and Dong had witnessed the whole incident and were just hoping and praying that Chang and Lee were still alive. But there was no sign of movement from the rubble of the mountain. They assumed that Chang and Lee were dead and sadly turned to leave, when they heard a sound of rocks being moved. They all quickly spun around. There was Chang and Lee digging themselves out from under the rocks and stones. They were overcome with joy; Black Beauty neighed excitedly and Ding and Dong barked, jumped, and wagged their tails. Chang and Lee were alive!

When Chang and Lee were free of the rubble, the Sapphire gem and the stone were in Chang's hands. Lee looked perfectly fine, but Chang's clothes were torn, and his body was covered with scars and bruises; he was also bleeding.

Only when they reached the other side of the forest where Black Beauty, Ding, and Dong were did Lee notice Chang's badly beaten-up body. Lee dashed back to the snow and picked up a mouthful. He rushed back and let the snow, which was now water, drip onto Chang's scars and bruises. After several trips back and forth, Chang was fully healed. They camped fifty meters away from the snow, but it was still cold because the wind from the snowy parts was blowing their way. Chang was tired and so exhausted, and his body was in pain from battling the dragon and fighting his way out from under the crumbled mountain. When Chang finally lapsed into sleep, he looked like a dead person.

Lee was also beat, and he too wanted to sleep, but he couldn't. He had to keep an eye out for anyone or any creature that might approach them. Just then, Ding and Dong awoke from their slumber and were prancing around energetically.

Lee got an idea. "Ding and Dong, do you think you can protect us while I am sleeping—because I am wiped out?"

"Sure," Ding and Dong both replied, running around in circles, thrilled that Lee trusted them with such an important job. When they turned back around to ask Lee exactly what to do, he was already fast asleep.

Ding said to Dong, "Well, he said that we must keep watch so if you see anything that looks suspicious, just growl and make your hair stand up and do some of the other scary and disgusting things you like to do."

"Okay, you mean that I should fart?" Dong asked.

"No! Just get to work!" Ding exclaimed.

Ding and Dong patrolled the whole night until Dong spotted a baby mouse and started to bark. Ding ran up to Dong and asked, "What is it?"

Dong just kept on barking at the same spot.

When Ding saw what he was barking at, he closed Dong's mouth with both his paws and shouted, "I told you to bark at animals and other creatures that are dangerous—not a baby mouse!"

"You never know…" Dong said.

"You never know what?" Ding said, perturbed.

"What if it is a dark force, pretending to be a baby mouse?" Dong said ominously.

"You know what? I never thought of that." Ding bumped his brother admiringly.

Once they were sure the mouse was no threat, they went back to patrolling throughout the night.

When morning arrived, they were still vigilantly patrolling. Lee kept on telling them they could stop, but they wouldn't listen.

Lee finally got tired of trying to call them off and went over to Chang. "Take out the map, please."

Chang produced the map and noticed that the Sapphire Dragon was gone. The only creature that remained was the Diamond Dragon. The biggest dragon out of all of them. He showed the map to Lee.

Lee looked at the map carefully then asked, "Chang, are you ready to slay this dragon?"

"Maybe," Chang mumbled.

"What do you mean *maybe?*"

"I mean the other four dragons I killed were all the same size, but the Diamond Dragon is double the size of all of them," Chang worried.

"But I am sure that you are looking forward to slaying your last dragon and saying good-bye to this magical forest?" Lee offered.

"To tell you the truth," Chang said, "I'm not really excited about slaying such a big dragon, and I will miss the forest. I kind of want to slay my last dragon, but frankly, I am nervous."

"Chang, you need to slay this dragon and get the last piece of the stone and the last gem, and it will be over, and no more killing," Lee said emphatically.

"But..." Chang began.

"Chang," Lee interjected, "do it for us, do it for me, do it for everyone, do it for Shanghai, and do it for China."

"Fine! I will do it!'" Chang exclaimed.

"That's my boy," Lee said. "Shall we get going?"

"Yes." Chang nodded.

Chang whistled for Ding and Dong to come over to him. The wolves stopped running in circles and looked dizzy; they both barked and fell to the ground.

"Am I the only one seeing stars?" Ding asked.

"No, I'm with you, brother, I, too, am seeing stars," Dong said.

After a while, they got up and ran to Chang.

"Are you done messing around?" he chided them.

"Yes," Ding and Dong said.

The Diamond Dragon

As usual, they followed the same routine in traveling to another destination. They ran and ran without stopping until the sky changed and wore a pink and orange coat. They came to a halt, and Chang took out the map and studied it. He saw the nearest destination was a small jungle of bamboo where there was a cave. Chang told Lee about their destination.

They ran and ran until the sky changed into its coat of stars. They kept running and the sky yet again changed into a pitch-black coat. Chang and the rest of them had been running for a very long time; the one thing he'd forgotten to do was to measure the distance to that small jungle.

They came to a halt and Lee asked, "How long did you say it was it to the bamboo jungle?"

"I didn't say how long it was until we reached the bamboo jungle." Chang shrugged.

"Well, take out the map and see how much longer it is until we reach there!" Lee snapped.

Chang quickly retrieved the map and looked at the small bamboo jungle then looked at where they were.

He put the map away with a frighten grin on his face and said, "Funny thing is, we're still a day away from the jungle."

Lee was so furious that he pounced on Chang, and when he did so, the boy fell off Black Beauty. Lee was growling at Chang and said, "I didn't teach you for nothing! I taught everything I knew to you and this how you are acting? You are busy playing daft with me, but I didn't teach you to be a stupid person!" Lee snapped. "You need to pull up your socks and start being mature like how I taught you!" Lee put his nose up against Chang's nose. "Do you understand me?"

"Yes," Chang muttered under his breath.

"Do you understand me?" Lee repeated, louder this time.

"Yes," Chang cried.

Lee got off Chang and walked away. The boy slowly got up from the ground and went to Black Beauty. Chang jumped on his horse, and they ran and ran until the sky yet again changed its coat into an orange one. They kept on running while the sky changed into a dark gray and fluffy coat.

They ran and ran until the sky began to cry and scream, but they still continued running, no matter what, even though Ding, Dong, and Black Beauty were scared of the screaming sky, their ears being very sensitive.

Lee felt nothing and heard nothing; he kept running with a stern face until the sky quit crying and screaming. They stopped just short of the bamboo jungle. Before

Lee entered, he changed himself into a panda, as did Ding and Dong.

Chang asked, "Lee, why did you, Ding, and Dong, change into panda bears?"

"Well," Lee explained, "pandas easily get frightened, and they can sense everything. But they don't know when you are a different creature. I disguised us so we don't spook them. They are very shy creatures, so if they sense some other creature is coming, they hide."

"Oh." Chang got it.

They all walked into the jungle, and at first there were no panda bears in sight. But as they walked farther into the jungle, panda bears started to stick their heads out to see who it was. When they saw three of their own kind, they all came out of the trees. As they were walking, a young panda bear slipped and fell from one of the bamboo trees, landing in front of Black Beauty.

Black Beauty was so frightened she lifted her front legs and neighed like crazy. The young panda bear was equally frightened, and it ran deeper into the bamboo jungle. Black Beauty became calm and all the panda bears emerged from the bamboo trees.

The biggest panda bear of them all approached and inquired, "What brings you here, fellow relatives?"

Lee spoke up. "We have traveled from a far place, and we come here to rest in the cave that lies within this jungle."

"You are welcome to stay in the cave that lies within our forest, but what may be your names?" the biggest panda asked.

"I am Lee, and these two cubs are Ding and Dong," Lee introduced them.

"What about the human and the horse?" the big panda asked.

"This is Chang who is on a special journey, and this is his trusty horse, Black Beauty," Lee replied.

"Nice to meet all of you. My name is Zhu, which means *bamboo* in Chinese," he said. "This is my family. Each panda in our family were found and brought to this magnificent jungle. We mostly eat bamboo, but I am not sure if Chang and his horse are able to eat it."

"That is true," Lee agreed.

"But don't worry, there is a small sugarcane patch near the cave that you wanted to stay in," Zhu said, turning. "Follow me and I will lead you to the cave."

Zhu walked ahead and showed them to their cave. When they stopped, Zhu apologized, "Sorry for frightening your horse. My cub, Ling, never stays in her den. I tell her lazy brother, Ying, to keep an eye on her, but he always falls asleep, and she runs off and does her thing."

"No, it is fine. I mean, she is still little and a lot of cubs are very adventurous and want to see everything and do everything," Lee said with a smile.

"I know," Zhu chuckled. "But here is your cave, and over there is the patch of sugarcane." He pointed with his nose. "Have a pleasant night."

"You too," Lee and Chang said together.

When they walked in, Chang marveled. "This cave is quite big."

"Chang, we won't change back into our normal selves until we are out of the bamboo jungle," Lee explained. "Only then can we change back."

"Okay by me," Chang said, "but I'm hungry."

"Go get some sugarcane to eat while I go get Ding, Dong, and I some bamboo to eat—and don't forget some sugarcane for Black Beauty too," Lee admonished.

"I won't!" Chang left the cave as did Lee. Black Beauty, Ding, and Dong were alone in the cave.

Ding said, "I wonder if Black Beauty talks?"

"Let's find out," Dong suggested.

They talked to Black Beauty, but all they heard back was neighing. Ding huffed, "Well, she doesn't talk, that sucks."

They lay there quietly when Chang came back to the cave with sugarcane in his hands. He split the cane between Black Beauty and himself.

Dong lifted his head and asked, "Where is Lee with the bamboo?"

"I don't know," Chang said, picking his teeth.

"What do you mean?"

"Exactly what it means," Chang replied, still picking his teeth.

An hour later, Lee came back. Ding and Dong got up, looked at Lee, and asked together, "What took you so long?"

"Zhu was talking to me and invited me into his den. I tried to excuse myself, but he wouldn't listen. I am sorry," Lee apologized.

He put the bamboo on the ground, and Ding and Dong ate heartily. Lee joined them while Chang and

Black Beauty were fast asleep. After they all ate, Ding and Dong quickly fell asleep. Lee was awake, but he was tired and felt sure this place was safe to stay, and so he fell asleep too. The sky was wearing its beautiful galaxy of stars and twinkling like glitter.

The next morning, the sky changed its coat to an orange, pink, and blue coat with half a mango coming up. Lee was the first one awake, then Ding, Dong, and Black Beauty. Chang was still fast asleep. They soon got hungry and went to get bamboo while Black Beauty waited for Chang to get up.

After an hour went by, the three panda bears who were originally a tiger and two wolves came back to the cave and had eaten, and Black Beauty had not. She was extremely hungry and waited, but then Lee went out the cave and soon came back with loads of sugarcane. Black Beauty ate the sugarcane but left some for Chang, who finally got up and finished it off. They departed from the cave and went all the way back to the entrance of the jungle. When they arrived, they tried to walk through the same way they came in, but there was some type of shield that prevented them from leaving.

Zhu showed up and said, "Don't you know that you can never exit the way you came in? You have to exit through the other side of the jungle."

"How long will that take?" Chang asked.

"If you are running, about half a day. If you are walking, one day. But my suggestion to you is to walk because there are creepy things back there." Zhu motioned over his shoulder. "Once, a long time ago, an adventurous panda bear went deeper into this jungle and was never to be seen again."

"Okay," Chang nodded.

"Have a safe trip," Zhu cautioned.

"That spoils our plan of exiting through the way we came in," Lee muttered under his breath.

"What was that?" Zhu asked.

"Nothing!" Lee said quickly.

Chang jumped on Black Beauty, and they ran all the way to the back of the forest, where they slowed and started to walk. This side of the forest was dark, damp, and scary. They proceeded very carefully so they wouldn't step on any rose jags.

Lee explained, "Rose jags are magical thorns which disguise themselves as roses. So if you touch them, they shoot poisonous thorns at you and you'll die immediately, and then they eat you."

It was so creepy that Black Beauty kept turning her head from side to side with a look of fright on her face. And then there was a two-headed frog that hopped past them. They walked for a whole day and finally came to the end of jungle and were able to exit. Lee, Ding, and Dong instantly changed back into their original selves. They hadn't seen the sky's coat for so long. It was now wearing a pitch-black coat and there was only one star. Where were all the others? They did not know. Since they were so tired of traveling, they walked only a little farther then camped for the night. Chang was bored and took out the map.

Lee asked, "So how many days until we get there?"

"I'd say about another three days or so," Chang estimated.

"But are you ready?" Lee looked at him quizzically.

"Kind of," Chang said. "Are you sure this is my last dragon I am going to slay?"

"I am sure about it," Lee said with an unsure face. "Chang, take out the four gems and the four pieces of the stone."

Chang did as he was told; he removed all the gems and the pieces of the stone and gently laid them down.

Lee looked at them and said, "Put the pieces of the stone in order."

Chang did so and it was shaped like a diamond, but there was no piece in the middle. That piece was with the Diamond Dragon.

"Now, Chang, can you see the gems look the same but with a different color and with different names?" Lee pointed out.

"Yes."

"Well, if you look carefully, you will see each dragon's face appear on one stone." Lee indicated with his paw.

Chang looked carefully, and to his surprise, there was indeed one dragon on each gem! Chang put the pieces of the stone back and the gems and lay on his grass mat.

Lee said, "Chang, you are still my little boy. Even though I am a tiger, you still belong to me."

"I know." Chang smiled.

"You better get to sleep because tomorrow is going to be a long day for everyone," Lee advised.

"Good night," Chang murmured.

When morning arrived, Lee was awake and so were the others. They were packed and ready to leave for their next destination.

Lee called out, "Chang, where shall our destination be for today?"

Chang removed the map and studied it. He traced his finger along the route and met with a place that was only a day away. Chang was sure that Lee wouldn't mind and reported, "Master Lee, the destination we are traveling to is one day away and is quite near to the Diamond Dragon."

"What is it?"

"It's a spring," Chang replied.

"Put the map away and jump on Black Beauty so that we can reach that spring by nightfall," Lee commanded.

Chang sprang into action, and in no time, they were on their way. The sky was not wearing its dark gray fluffy coat, but rather a beautiful blue coat with a huge mango sitting there and shining like a golden ball. They ran and ran; the sun's rays were strong, and Chang was sweating like a pig. He couldn't imagine how hot all these animals felt because they had fur on their bodies. Even though he was extremely thirsty, he stopped thinking about the hot weather and was only thinking of how he was going to slay the Diamond Dragon in the next two days. Chang only wished that he had the power to kill that dragon in one shot with one of those contraptions that shot gunpowder out of a nozzle. But he always wished for an adventure like this. His master always told him to be careful with what he wishes for, but he never listened; he just thought that it was a bunch of nonsense. Now he knew that the wish that he wished for when he was eight years old had actually come true. The sky was now wearing its orange and pink coat; they were still traveling when Chang halted Black Beauty. Lee also stopped and so did Ding and Dong.

Lee asked, "What is the matter, Chang?"

"I'm feeling so tired and clammy," Chang panted.

"Chang, there is only another three hours till we get there, and then you can drink as much water as you want," Lee said.

"Fine," Chang sighed.

And so they carried on running for the next three hours.

When they sky yet again changed and wore a beautiful coat full of twinkling stars, they had finally arrived at the spring. Chang made a fire and took a dip in the spring; he drank so much that he finished one full bottle of water. Chang lay on his grass mat and looked at the sky. He saw a shooting star and closed his eyes and made a wish. He then fell asleep without saying good night to any of them; in fact, he was the only one to sleep.

Dong asked, "What was that shiny thing that shot across the sky?"

"A star," Lee answered.

"Then why was it moving?" Dong wondered.

"It is a shooting star. If you wish on one, your dreams might come true—but you can't tell anyone," Lee explained.

"Lee, can we patrol tonight?" Ding asked, jumping up and down with excitement.

"No!" Lee exclaimed then said in a quieter voice, "I mean, no, I shall patrol tonight."

"Okay," Ding said.

"Lee, can we come with you when you are killing the dragon?" Dong asked.

"No," Lee said.

"Why?" Ding and Dong asked.

"You need to protect Black Beauty while we are in there," Lee said.

"But we want to see what a dragon looks like," Ding said wistfully.

"Well, they are big and scary," Lee warned.

"We know that," Ding said. "We want to see what a dragon looks like anyway."

"Well, maybe some other time, but if you don't go to bed, I will get the tickling fuzzy tiger," Lee said.

Ding and Dong immediately fell to the ground and slept. Lee looked at Black Beauty, who put her head down and fell asleep.

The next morning, when everyone was awake, they packed everything. Chang jumped on Black Beauty, and they started to run. The sky was not wearing its blue coat with a huge mango on it; instead it was wearing a black fluffy coat. They came to a halt when they saw a cave. Chang took out the map and looked at where they were they were compared to the place where the Diamond Dragon was.

Chang said in confusion, "Master Lee, how is it possible that we reached the Diamond Dragon now and not tomorrow?"

"I do not know. You are the one who estimated the distance of how far away we were," Lee said.

"But I estimated the distance properly," Chang insisted.

He then looked at the map again and saw that the distance was right, but maybe he forgot and meant to say something else. Chang said, "I think I was supposed to say that we were two days away from the Diamond Dragon."

"That is why I don't trust you when it comes to maps, but I leave it." Lee shook his head.

Chang jumped off Black Beauty, put the map away, tied her to a tree, and told Ding and Dong, "You two need to stay here and guard while we go inside. We won't be long."

They both agreed. Chang took his sword and entered the cave with Lee. At the entrance of the cave there was a fire torch. Chang took it and they continued on. They were amazed with the walls, which were studded with diamonds. They realized that they were inside a diamond mine.

Lee said, "This diamond mine was said to be destroyed. It is the biggest diamond mine in the world, and it was abandoned two hundred years ago."

"How do you know?" Chang asked.

"Before I was a human, I was a dragon myself. I lived in this very cave with my dragon mother. When people found this mine and found us, they killed us and used us for all sorts of things," Lee said.

"Oh," Chang marveled.

"But then they abandoned this place. They said that this forest was a creepy place, and this mine was haunted by ghosts. But meanwhile, it was baby dragon and that baby dragon turned out to be the Diamond Dragon."

"You have so many fascinating stories that you didn't want to tell me, and you are telling me now when we are going to battle!" Chang exclaimed.

"Ssshhhh…" Lee whispered, "Chang, you need to keep your voice down, otherwise the dragon will hear you, and the diamonds above you have sharp ends and they can kill you."

"Oh," Chang said, looking above him.

The ceiling had diamonds, pointing down at them with a pointed end, which looked very sharp. They turned left and entered a huge place where the Diamond Dragon was sleeping. There were two pools of water that each looked like a diamond; they walked carefully and quietly down the pathway when a small diamond fell into the water. Luckily, the Diamond Dragon didn't open his eyes. They hurried down the pathway, and accidently, two medium-sized diamonds fell in each pool.

This time, the Diamond Dragon awakened, stood up on his feet, and asked, "Who disturbs me from my slumber?"

"It is I, Lee, and Chang," Lee announced.

"I see… I know that you have killed my brothers and my sister," the Diamond Dragon said.

"Y-yes, I have," Chang stammered.

"Well, this time it isn't going to be me who dies. It is both of you who will die," the Diamond Dragon roared and lashed his tail by Lee, but he dodged it.

Chang was near the dragon and stabbed his tail then climbed his back and stabbed him, but he didn't screech with pain. The wound that Chang made with his sword had healed. Chang kept on stabbing the Diamond Dragon with his sword, but it kept healing. Finally, the Diamond Dragon flung Chang to the wall of the mine while Lee continued battling him.

Chang was still sitting on the floor and shouted to Lee, "Everything that I try doing doesn't work. Every time I stab him, it heals."

"Even though I am a magical creature I can't defeat him either. He is way too powerful," Lee cried. "But there is a diamond sword that lies in this mine. You will have to go deeper into the mine and fetch it in order to kill him. You'll have to hurry because I can't keep distracting him too long, otherwise I will die."

Chang got off the floor and dashed past the dragon and through an entrance. The pathway was dark, but his sword was glowing so bright that it was his light to guide him safely along the path. He ran faster; it seemed like the tunnel went on forever, but then Chang came to an end. And there it was: the solid diamond sword, laying on the rock, glistening so bright it almost blinded Chang The only thing preventing him from getting to it was a huge gap filled with water, and he couldn't go around. He tried to think of a way and remembered that he couldn't take too long to figure this out; he needed to come up with something quick.

He then thought of an idea that might kill him, but he had to chance it. There were two tall and large diamond pillars that looked like they would shatter if they fell. He used his sword to loosen the left diamond pillar. It fell and shattered, but it didn't break into pieces; there were circles of diamonds floating that looked like a bridge but without any handholds.

Chang left his sword on the ground and hopped onto the first diamond. He nearly fell but kept his balance; he hopped to the next and to the next until he was standing on the last one, where he took one giant leap and landed on the other side safely. He walked carefully, climbed the steps, and had gently removed the sword from its place when there was a sudden rumble beneath his feet. He turned around and saw that the circles were starting to fall. He ran and jumped on the first and then the next and the next.

When he reached the last one, he took a big leap but didn't manage to make it. Chang held on tightly to the edge with his right hand and the sword in his left. He brought his left hand up and placed it on the ground and reached as far as he could then pulled himself up quickly. As soon as he was on terra firma, he picked up both swords and ran back up to where the dragon was.

Chang threw his own sword aside and stabbed the dragon with the diamond sword. The dragon screeched with pain this time, and Chang climbed his back and stabbed him. The dragon flung Chang off his back. Chang had noticed the dragon had a stinger at the end of his tail, and he had an idea. Chang stood under the dragon's stomach and punched away. The dragon tried to use his stinger to sting Chang—instead he stung himself. Chang then climbed on his back and stabbed him. Again the dragon screeched with pain and Chang climbed his neck, wrapped his legs tightly around it and stabbed him in his head. The dragon finally fell to the ground. Lee ripped the stone from his neck.

Chang dug the gem out of the armor using the diamond stone. The roof above them started to collapse, and the diamond daggers from the ceiling began to fall. Chang took both swords and the two of them ran out. Before they got to the exit, one of the daggers went into Chang's, skin but there was no time, and they hurried outside. When they turned around and looked, the Diamond Dragon was gone.

Journey Back Home

Now that all the dragons were killed and everything was collected, the gems and the pieces of the stone. The next step was to retrieve the lost treasure of Shanghai.

Chang was badly bruised and scarred. The diamond dagger that got stuck in his arm was still there. When he removed the dagger from his arm, it was bleeding, and he was in extreme pain. Lee took the dagger from Chang's hand and put it in the spring that was nearby; he then collected water in his mouth and poured it all over Chang until there were no scars and bruises except the place where the dagger had stuck. It had left a terrible scar on his arm.

Chang got off the ground, and they walked to Black Beauty and Ding and Dong. Chang untied Black Beauty from the tree, and they camped there for the night. He was so exhausted that he was the first one to sleep. Lee too was exhausted, and before he fell asleep, he asked Ding and Dong to do guard duty. They happily agreed, and later Black Beauty fell asleep. The only two creatures that were awake were Ding and

Dong. They were going in circles around their area and making sure nothing happened. They soon got dizzy and went for a drink of water. When they came back to resume patrolling, something didn't seem right. They sensed that an unwanted mythical creature had passed by them without being invited. They wanted to go and investigate, but they were ordered to guard.

"How are we supposed to see what came by?" Dong proposed. "Maybe it stole something valuable, like a gem? Surely nothing else will happen."

Ding had paid attention to Lee and knew the answer. "We have to put up a shield, Dong."

"But how?"

"I'm pretty sure we just both bark at the same time," Ding theorized.

They gave it a try, and *voila*...an invisible shield was there.

"Now, surely nothing will happen," Ding concluded.

They walked and sniffed until they reached a very dark area. Ding and Dong heard noises like howling and barking and sneaked up to the entrance of a huge cave. Inside, many werewolves, standing on two feet, were admiring something shiny one held in his hands. It was the diamond sword.

Ding and Dong entered and the howling and barking stopped as the werewolves turned around and looked at them.

The one holding the sword said, "Well, boys, look what we have here...puppies."

"Have you lost your mother?" another werewolf teased.

"We can look after ourselves. Now give us back the sword!" Ding shouted.

"A very grumpy puppy, too," one of them remarked.

"You want it, come get it," one holding the sword challenged.

The werewolves laughed and laughed. Ding and Dong got so irritated and barked so loud that the earth rumbled beneath the werewolves' feet.

"That's just for starters," Ding threatened.

The werewolves were completely surprised by the powers of these "puppies" and quickly gave up the sword. Ding took it in his teeth, and along with Dong, they marched back to the campsite. They entered the shield, put the sword down, and fell asleep. That was not quite an adventure, but they'd figured out their abilities.

The next morning, Chang got up and started to walk to the spring when he hit the shield. He kept on touching until he became exasperated and woke Lee up.

Lee said, "Chang, I can't get rid of this shield. The only creatures that might have created the shield must have been Ding and Dong."

They looked at Ding and Dong who were sleeping. Five minutes later, Ding and Dong woke up and yawned. Chang was leaning on the shield when both Ding and Dong barked together. The shield disappeared and Chang fell down.

Lee asked, "So where did you two scoundrels go to last night?"

"Well, we sensed that some creature came here, and we put a shield on you guys so nothing could hurt you," Dong said. "We went off to find out. We saw a cave full of werewolves who had the diamond sword. We got it back and came here and left the shield up."

"What he said," Ding confirmed.

Lee just shook his head then turned to Chang who had picked himself up and was dusting himself off. "Chang, how far is it until we get home?"

"Well, it should take us the same amount of time as we came," Chang replied.

"Chang, remember, we can't exit the way we came in. You can only exit through a way you never came through, and if you open the map you will see something," Lee suggested.

Chang took out the map and saw that it was now a different map. It only had the place where they were currently at and there was an exit, but no land— just water.

Chang put the map away and asked, "How are we supposed to get back home if there is only water between here and there?"

"You'll see," Lee smiled mysteriously. "Just pack up and jump on that horse so we can get to our destination."

"Okay." Chang did as he was told.

"But we are tired," Ding and Dong moaned.

"Well, go drink some water," Lee said.

Ding and Dong went to drink. Chang was on Black Beauty waiting for Ding and Dong to finish getting some water. Chang asked Lee, "Why are they taking so long?"

"They said that they were tired, and I told them to go and drink water…" Lee whispered, "as a distraction."

"Don't they have those powers that help you boost your energy?" Chang asked, surprised.

"No, they are still too young to have those abilities. But they may get some of their powers that they were supposed to have later on now," Lee said.

"Oh."

Ding and Dong finished drinking the water from the spring and came over to Chang and Lee. They said they now had enough energy and started to run north. They ran and ran without stopping, but they didn't know how far the end of the forest was. They just kept running aimlessly until the sky was wearing its star coat. The group stopped for moment and Lee asked, "How far is it until we get there?"

"I don't know," Chang shrugged.

"Then look," Lee growled.

Chang took out the map, traced his finger along the route, and stopped at where they were currently standing. He kept one finger on where they were and used his other finger to trace along the map until he got to the end of the forest and estimated. "Lee, it is going to take us one week to get there."

"That is too long for me, but there is solution," Lee responded.

"What?"

"I have a roar that can make us all disappear and then reappear somewhere else...problem is, I don't know where."

"Isn't that a bit risky?"

"It may also take us backward instead of forward." Lee cautioned.

"What then?" Chang worried.

"Wait a minute," Lee corrected himself. "It can't take us backward, it will only take us forward. The route we are traveling on is north, right? So if I roar, we will still be traveling north, but in a different location."

"If you're sure about it…" Chang said uneasily.

"Trust me," Lee firmly said. "Just stand together real tight so that all of us can be transported to another destination."

They all huddled close together, and Lee roared loudly. They had disappeared from where they were and reappeared in another location. Chang took out the map and followed his finger along the route and saw that they were now only five days away. "Lee, you need to roar one more time so we can get there faster."

"You better be right this time, and when we are home, I am sleeping as long as I want, because I have been playing night guard for over four months in this forest," Lee snapped.

They followed the same procedure, and Lee roared again. They all disappeared and reappeared, this time at the end of the forest. There was huge ocean of water that never ended.

"So how are we supposed to get home without a means of transport?" Chang fretted.

Lee simply smiled.

Moments later, a huge ship rose up from beneath the water. At the bow of the ship was a dragon head. There was a ramp leading onto the boat, and they went up it. As soon as they were on board the ship, the ramp disappeared.

The boat started to sink and Chang was getting worried, but Lee looked unconcerned. Before they could go down, Chang shouted in a panic, "We need to get off this boat!"

"Relax," Lee said calmly, "it is going take us home."

Chang coaxed himself to relax, and they were soon under the water and gone from the forest, never to return again. Just as quickly as it had sunk, the boat came up to the surface. They were all soaking wet, and Chang looked grumpy because he had a catfish in his mouth. Chang tried to talk, but all they heard was groaning and mumbling coming out.

Lee said, "Let me get that for you."

Lee went over and took the catfish out of Chang's mouth and kept it in his own mouth.

Chang stuck out his tongue in disgust and said, "Thank you. But now my breath smells like fish and seawater."

The Chamber

They walked off the boat, and it immediately disappeared beneath the water. Chang was so pleased to be home that he actually went down on his knees and kissed the ground.

An hour later, when he entered the house, it was full of dust and spider webs he'd have to clean.

But Lee came in and said, "Don't worry, Chang, I will get this place sparkling clean so that you don't have to." Lee roared once and the place was sparkling clean.

Chang ran upstairs and took a bath. He came back down fresh and clean then made a fire outside and roasted the catfish. He gave Black Beauty some fruit to eat, and they drank from the waterfall. Chang put Black Beauty in a small house -like barn, which was just big enough for her. He brought her grass and water and left two windows open. He went inside to his bedroom, Lee went to his old bedroom downstairs, and Ding and Dong went to Chang's room. Chang made a bed of blankets for both of them to sleep on. Chang jumped into his bed and soon fell asleep, feeling good. He had left the pieces of the stone, the gems, his sword, and the diamond sword in a downstairs room. Chang felt sure that everyone was safe because Lee had put a shield around their house and Black Beauty's small house as well.

The next morning, when the sky had changed into its dark-grey fluffy coat, Lee removed the shields from both of the houses.

Soon Chang was bored. "Master Lee, what could we do now?"

"Well, why don't you go grab the map for getting into the chamber?" Lee suggested.

Chang got out of bed, went to his dresser, took the map out from his cupboard, and came back and sat down on the bed again. He opened it and saw that there were so many tunnels, routes, and pathways for getting through the place where he had to go to find the lost treasure of Shanghai. Chang was so looking forward to getting there and chirped, "Master Lee, can we go to the chamber today?"

"Be patient…it is too soon. We need to wait for a while," Lee cautioned.

Chang let out a sigh of exasperation.

"But I want you to bring the pieces of the stone and the gems to me. Leave the map here because we have a lot to do today," Lee said.

Chang went to various places to get the pieces of the stone and the gems. One by one, he brought all the things that he was asked to and laid them on the floor of his bedroom in front of Lee.

"We first have to figure out a route to get to the right path." Lee explained.

"Well, how are we supposed to get there when there are so many routes, pathways, and other things that lead it to it?" Chang said, bewildered.

"No," Lee corrected him, "the map is tricking you into thinking that you can take any pathway or route, and it will lead you straight there. No, there is one route that will take us there, but we have to do this wisely."

"Don't we need a pencil to remember our route?"

"No," Lee shook his head. "We don't. We need to remember this route because if we write on this map, it will disappear as soon as we enter the cave. Plus, since you have three magical creatures around you, they will pick it up, and as soon as you put the map away, the lines will go away."

"Oh," Chang said.

They studied the routes and the pathways carefully to choose the right one. There were five pathways and five routes. They spent the whole day looking at the map until their eyes were getting strained from looking so close. But when the sun began to set, Lee looked closer at the map and saw that one of the paths had a shadow. He got the boy's attention and told him, "Chang, you need to remember this pathway. It is the fourth pathway to the left and, Ding, Dong, you too need to remember this path—remember, it is the fourth pathway to the left."

"Okay!" exclaimed Chang, Ding, and Dong.

They put the map away, and Chang put everything else where he previously had it and came back to his room. "Now that we know which route to take, how long must we wait to go to the chamber?"

Lee gave it some thought then replied, "We must wait three more days because we have a lot of things to do and tomorrow we start."

"What is it?" Chang asked.

"I will tell you tomorrow," Lee replied. "Go get us some dinner because I am starving."

"Okay," Chang said and went outside. He took his fishing pole, which was made out of bamboo with a string and a hook. He had just started to fish when he got a bite. Chang had a tough battle of getting the fish out of the water, but eventually, he reeled in a giant catfish. It was a beautiful, plump, juicy piece of fish.

They cooked the fish and ate it. Lee put the shields on, and they went to bed.

The next morning, Chang was ready and sitting in Lee's room. He asked Lee when he woke up, "So what stuff are we going to do today?"

"Okay, we need to go to the village and find a lady called Ling. And then we have to go find another lady, Lang," Lee said.

"Question," Chang spoke up. "Are they sisters?"

"No, they are not," Lee replied.

"Then why are we going to them?"

"Because, they are people who can help you and me. They can tell anything that you just did recently," Lee said.

"Do they know that the forest is magical?"

"Of course they know that the forest is magical. They were animals from that forest once, but then their own kind killed them and they came back in a reincarnation as these people who can tell anything and everything. But they are not Chinese. They are people who are called Americans," Lee said.

"Wow!" Chang exclaimed.

"But we have to leave now because a lot of Europeans sail here just to get to them," Lee said, getting a move on. "Chang, please would you get a small black bag from my drawer."

"Which drawer is it in?" Chang asked.

"The last drawer," Lee replied.

"What is it?" Chang asked.

"It is a magical bag," Lee replied.

Lee put a protective shield on both of the houses and took both Black Beauty and the wolves, and they left for the village. After fifteen minutes of walking, they arrived in the village. It had been long since Chang had been here. Chang remembered when he came to collect Black Beauty for his journey. They walked until they saw a place that had a blue awning with stars on it, and the windows were tinted so that no one could see inside. They tied Black Beauty to a post and asked a small Chinese boy with short black hair to watch her for a small fee.

They entered the place, and there was extreme silence and a strong smell of incense. Soon, a lady emerged from a back room. She had blond silky hair tied in a dark blue bandana riddled with stars. She had fair, smooth skin, her eyes were the same blue as the Sapphire Dragon's fire, her nails were on the long side and were painted black. She had a pointy nose and wore a long, silk moon dress that went all the way down to her ankles. She also had many rings on her fingers;

she wore black shoes and she had the pendant with the symbol of yin and yang around her neck. When she saw them, she quickly ran to the door and locked it and dragged them both into a back room, which was dimly lit.

She seated Chang down, hurried to her seat, looked into her crystal ball, and said, "I see that you have slain all five dragons in the magical forest, and you are headed to the chamber."

"We know that." Chang rolled his eyes.

"Chang, you have to be respectful to Ling," Lee reprimanded him.

Chang bowed his head as if to say "I'm sorry."

"My oh my, there is a special present waiting for you in the chamber, and it is something else other than the treasure," Ling said, still staring into the crystal ball.

"What is it?" Chang was bouncing in his seat.

"I cannot tell you that," Ling said mysteriously. "Now you need to get all these things for me and bring them back here tomorrow. I need a dragon's tooth, mermaid scales, tears of a werewolf, the eyeball of a lion, spit from a wolf, a piece of hair from a white horse, and a piece of your hair. You can get all those things from a man who lives in the rich part of our village called Shen. Here's the address, and I will see you tomorrow."

"Okay," Chang said, but he was not so sure.

She led them out the door and locked it behind them. Chang opened the black bag, and to his surprise he found enough money to pay the small boy thirty Chinese Yuan (which is equivalent to five US dollars) and took Black Beauty.

Chang then questioned Lee about this magical bag and Lee calmly replied that the bag will provide him with resources that he needs at short notice, but he cannot abuse its generosity.

They went to another part of the village to the lady called Lang, but she wasn't there, so they continued on to the rich part of the village where Shen lived. He was the same guy who Chang got Black Beauty from. They walked up a paved pathway and when they got to the top, Shen saw the boy on his horse and walked up to greet them.

"Haven't see you for a long while, Chang." Shen smiled, tipping his hat.

"Well, I had some things to do," Chang said.

When Shen looked toward the back of Black Beauty and saw Lee, he got such a fright and took off shouting, "Chang, run for your life! There is a tiger behind you!"

Shen stopped when he saw that Chang wasn't afraid. He then walked slowly toward Chang, hesitated, and asked, "Why aren't you running?"

"Because he's my pet…and actually my master," Chang replied.

"What do you mean?" Shen looked confused.

"This is Master Lee," Chang said proudly.

"But I thought he was dead?" Shen scratched his head.

"He was, but he came back in the reincarnation of a tiger—and he can talk too, listen…" Chang said excitedly.

"Hi, Shen," Lee said warmly. "I haven't seen you for long time."

Shen was in such shock that he fainted. Five minutes later, Shen came to. Lee was looking down at him with concern.

"Are you okay, Shen?"

"Y-yes, I am." Shen touched his forehead. "I think."

Lee stepped back and Shen got to his feet.

"What is the reason that you come here?" Shen said without asking any more questions.

Chang stepped forward. "We went to this lady called Ling and she gave us this list of things that she said you have."

"Show me the list." Shen held out his hand.

Chang found the list and gave it to Shen. He excused himself and went inside his house. Ten minutes later, he came back out with a bulging sack and said, "Here are all the things that you need."

"Thanks," Chang said, eagerly grabbing the bag and turning to leave.

"Where do you think you're going?" Shen stopped him. "You still have to pay me my money because those things are hard to get."

"Sorry," Chang replied.

"How much is it?" Chang asked.

"One thousand eight hundred Chinese Yuan" (three hundred US dollars) Shen replied.

Chang is shocked by the amount of money Shen is asking for. He looks to Lee, and Lee just smiles. Chang then reaches into the bag, and to his surprise, he is able to pull out the amount requested and then hands it to Shen.

Chang then tied the sack to Black Beauty and headed back to Ling. But Lee stopped him and advised him that "she said that we must come back to her tomorrow."

"But we got the things now," Chang protested. "We can give it to her today, and then we don't have to go back to her tomorrow."

"We can't," Lee insisted.

"Why not?"

"There is a reason she wants us to come tomorrow so let us go home," Lee said with finality.

"Okay," Chang replied. Disappointment was written all over his face.

They walked through the forest until they got home. Lee removed the shields and Chang took everything off Black Beauty that was tied to her inside the house then took her to her barn, gave her food and water, and let Lee put the invisible shield back on. Inside the house, he put the sack away in one of the kitchen cupboards and Ding and Dong ran up to Chang's room to sleep. Lee said, "Chang, why don't you go get us some noodles and banana leaves?"

Chang went outside and collected banana leaves, but where was he supposed to get noodles from? He went back inside and laid the banana leaves on the kitchen table.

He asked Lee, "Where am I supposed to get noodles?"

"From the village, of course," Lee said.

"But won't the places where they sell noodles be closed?" Chang put forward.

"No, there is one place in the village. She is an old lady who lives with her young daughter and her three grandchildren. They make noodles for a living and sell them to earn money. I used to buy from them, and they are open till late. Take one hundred thousand dong and go," Lee said.

Chang took the money and left the house, and fifteen minutes later, he arrived in the village. He kept looking until he saw a sign that said "Noodles for Sale."

The door was open, and there were candles lit and he could hear children laughing. He walked in the door and saw an old lady who was making noodles. He asked, "How much are the noodles?"

"One hundred thousand dong," the old lady replied.

Chang gave her the money, one of the children handed him the noodles, and Chang went back home.

He made a fire, put a metal grid on it that he'd made himself, put the noodles in the pot and onto the grid. He chopped the banana leaves into the noodles and waited for it to boil. He then served it to Lee and himself in bowls. He washed the dishes afterward, then put everything away, and put out the fire.

Lee put the shields up, and the two of them went inside the house and climbed into their beds.

The next morning, when everyone was up and assembled downstairs, Lee got rid of all the shields. Chang took the sack out of the kitchen cupboard and went outside; he put the saddle on Black Beauty then tied the sack to her while Lee put the shields on both houses and they left for the village.

Fifteen minutes later, they arrived at Ling's place. Chang tied Black Beauty to a post and asked the same little Chinese boy to watch her. He removed the sack, and when Chang and Lee entered the place, again there was a strong smell of incense. Ling came out of the back room, quickly locked the door, and motioned them to follow her.

Once inside the room she asked, "Do you have the things?"

"Yes, I do," Chang said with pride.

"Then give them to me,"

Chang handed Ling the sack; she took it and said, "Follow me."

They followed her into another room; it was the kitchen. She had blazing fire going with a big pot hanging over it. She said, "I will need some time—until tomorrow morning. You have to come in the early hours of the morning when it is still dark, then this drink will be ready. I will need a sample of your hair, please."

Chang plucked a strand of his hair and one of Lee's and gave it to her.

They left the place; Chang paid the little boy and untied Black Beauty. It was midday and they had nothing to do except go home.

When they arrived home, Lee removed the shields, Chang removed everything from Black Beauty and left her in her barn with food and water. Lee put a shield up, and they all went inside and up to Chang's room.

"Are we going to the chamber tomorrow?" Chang said anxiously.

"Yes, we are," Lee nodded.

"But how do we enter palace property without being recognized as trespassers by any of the guards?" Chang worried.

"There is a way—you'll see," Lee said.

"Okay," Chang said. "But must I take both swords?"

"No, you don't," Lee said.

"Which one should I take?"

"Take the normal one," Lee replied. "Now we need an early night, so let us all go to bed."

"But what about dinner?" Chang's stomach was growling.

"You can get breakfast in the morning, but right now, you need to get to bed while I put the shields on," Lee said.

"Okay, good night," Chang said reluctantly.

"Good night," Lee replied.

Chang went up to his bedroom and fell right to sleep. Lee put the shields on and went up to his bedroom and fell asleep as well.

When the early hours of the morning arrived, Chang was already in the kitchen gobbling down a big breakfast. Afterward, they packed everything on Black Beauty and made sure nothing important was left behind. Lee put the shields on, and they took off.

They arrived in the village and went to Ling's place. She took them to the kitchen, gave them the liquid, and said, "This potion that I made for you is for protection, healing, and strength. It only works for twelve hours so use it wisely. Good luck."

"Thank you very much," Chang said.

Chang opened the potion bottle, which gave off an awful stench, making him react by pulling an unpleasant facial expression. He drank half the potion and gave the balance to Lee.

They then left and walked and they walked, until they passed through the rich part of the village and continued farther into the even richer part until they saw the palace where the great Emperor Wong and the beautiful Princess Xueman lived.

Lee said, "Follow me."

Chang trailed Lee behind the palace where there was nothing but a long and high wall. But when Lee put his paw over a spot on the wall, a door appeared. They grabbed the pieces of the stone, the gems, and the sword. Lee ordered Black Beauty and Ding and Dong to stay behind and put them in a shield. Once Lee and Chang entered, the door disappeared.

Chang suggested, "Lee, how about you carry the pieces of the stone while I carry the gems and the sword?"

"Good idea, "Lee concurred.

Chang secured the sack with the pieces of the stone around Lee's neck, and he put the sack with the gems around his own neck and held his sword in his hand.

They began walking and soon came to a stop. There were ten pathways in front of them. Chang pointed and said, "Lee, remember we must take the pathway which is fourth to the left?""Oh, yes, thank you for reminding me," Lee said.

They entered that pathway and it led them to a cavernous area with two pools of lava along the side of the wide path. At first they thought they had reached the entrance, but they were greeted by a big surprise: a huge solid gold dragon who was asleep—and it was bigger than the Diamond Dragon.

The Golden Dragon awakened and saw Chang and Lee. "Why do you wish to enter here, for you have slain my children? And now I must have my revenge by taking both of your lives."

The Golden Dragon blew fire, but Chang was able to get under the dragon's stomach before it reached him. He stabbed it but to no avail because it wasn't flesh—it was solid gold.

"How am I supposed to slay it?" Chang wondered aloud. Then the solution came to mind as he thought quickly before the dragon could kill him. He dashed behind a boulder where he could see the lava and said to himself, "Lava can melt many things...including gold! But how am I supposed to get the lava?"

Lee called out to him, "Take your sword and dip the blade into the lava."

Chang did so, and it turned into a lava blade. Chang ran toward the dragon; he went under its stomach and stabbed him. This time, the dragon screeched in pain. Chang then climbed its back and went higher to its neck and shouted, "I deserve to live, and you deserve to die!"

Chang took his lava sword and slashed the dragon's head off then quickly jumped off the dragon's back. The body of the dragon fell into the lava, and immediately, the lava overflowed and was coming right at them. Lee roared, and an invisible shield popped up and protected them from the surging lava.

After five minutes, the lava dried up, and Lee removed the shield. A door had opened when the Golden Dragon died, and they quickly ran inside. They were finally in the chamber! At last they had found it!

"But where is the treasure?" Chang cried.

Lee said, "Chang, take the sack with the stone pieces. There were six dragons in a diamond shape. And there was one in the middle that had the place to put the pieces of the stone together."

Chang did as he was instructed.

Lee continued, "Put the stone pieces together first then put the gems in the mouths of the dragon gargoyles."

"Okay," Chang said and began laying the stones out on the floor.

The chamber was huge and dimly lit and damp. It had moss, and the walls were green. Chang put the pieces of the stone in order and then took each gem out, the emerald gem for the Emerald Dragon, the coral gem for the Coral Dragon, the moonstone gem for the Moonstone Dragon, the sapphire gem for the Sapphire Dragon, and the diamond gem for the Diamond Dragon. Once he placed all the gems in mouths of the dragon gargoyles, a blue beam of light sprang forth. It became a diamond shape and had a line going vertically and another line horizontally. Just then, a wind came up and the spirits of the dragon spun in circles around Chang and went into their gems.

Arrested

The dragon in the middle started to go up then stopped a metre away from them, and there it was—the true lost treasure of Shanghai that had been missing for so long. The treasure was a golden Buddha that had a crystal ball with all the gems on it. Chang took it and put it in his sack. In the next moment, a door opened in front of them that led into the palace.

They entered the room where the so-called treasure was kept. Chang walked up to the fake treasure and took it out of its place. He was putting the real one where the fake used to be when Emperor Wong entered and saw Chang.

The emperor shouted, "Thief! Thief!"

The guards came immediately and Emperor Wong bellowed, "Arrest him…and take his tiger too!"

They arrested Chang and Lee, put them in shackles, and led them away to the dungeon.

When Princess Xueman came to see why her father had cried out, she saw Chang and then looked at the treasure. She was sure that she'd seen that piece somewhere and ran to her room.

When Chang and Lee were thrown in the dungeon, they were surprised to see Black Beauty and Ding and Dong in there, wearing shackles as well. Chang shook his head in disbelief. "How did you get here when you were protected by the shield?"

"Well, when we saw the guards, we started to bark," Ding explained. "We couldn't help ourselves."

"How are we supposed to get out of here?" Chang moaned.

Later in the evening, Princess Xueman found the book she was looking for and quickly opened it. She saw the same piece that she'd seen when she came to see why her father was upset in the treasure room.

She rushed to the emperor's room and cried out, "Father, that boy and his tiger aren't thieves. They were retrieving the real lost treasure of Shanghai."

"What do you mean?" Emperor Wong looked at his daughter warily.

"Father, look…this book says that piece is the true lost treasure of Shanghai, see…" Princess Xueman handed her father the book.

Emperor Wong took the book, looked at it carefully, then shouted, "Guards! Guards! Bring the prisoners to me at once!"

Five minutes later, Chang, Lee, Black Beauty, Ding, and Dong were brought before the emperor. He told the guards, "Release them."

The guards removed the shackles at once, and the five former prisoners were overcome with joy.

Emperor Wong addressed them. "I do apologize, and I thank you for retrieving the lost treasure of Shanghai. What do you want in return? Ask and it is yours."

Chang thought for a moment then replied, "I wish to be your royal advisor, to live in the palace, and for my animals to live in the palace as well."

"Done and done," Emperor Wong smiled. "Welcome to the palace."

And so that is how Chang moved into the palace and became the royal advisor. Chang was indeed happy to have everyone around him—his master, Lee, his animals, and his new friend, the princess. But most of all, he enjoyed his adventure, and I also hope that you did too…

Also by Kiara Loganathan

The Goblin King and the Rare Dragonfly
ISBN 13   Softcover: 978-1-4653-0359-2